MW01169374

PURE AS SNOW

LAURA BURTON
JESSIE CAL

COPYRIGHT

The characters and storylines are fictitious, and any resemblance to real-life people and events are purely coincidental. The author retains all of the rights to this work which may not be copied and distributed online or elsewhere without the written permission of the owner of the rights.

All rights reserved by Laura Burton and Jessie Cal 2021.

Published by Burton & Burchell Ltd
To discuss rights:
Laura@burtonburchell.co.uk

First Edition

Edited by Susie Poole

CHAPTER ONE

Snow White hugged her knees and counted back from one hundred with her eyes closed. She hated dark, enclosed spaces. She gritted her teeth, trying to ignore the emotions raging in her chest. Her sister, Aria, had turned into a cold-hearted monster, also known as The Snow Queen. But Snow never imagined Aria would throw her own sister in the dungeon.

Perhaps Aria didn't expect Snow to turn on her, either. But one thing was clear: the two sisters had changed.

The image of George being thrown into the lake was burned in her memory and played on a loop whenever she was in the dark. She took a deep, shaking breath and listened to the steady drip echoing in the cell. Snow had no conceivable idea of what wretched plans The Snow Queen had for her after what she'd done. She was capable of murder, and that knowledge was enough to convince her that she wasn't going to be a sitting duck and wait for her evil sister to return.

The welcome flap of wings lit up Snow's dark mood, and she opened her eyes, blinking in the dim cell just as Roger, her white barn owl, swooped in. A brass key dropped in her hands as he flew over her head, and he settled on the damp floor beside her.

"You are so clever. Thank you, Roger," Snow said, smoothing his back feathers with her index finger.

Aria has left the castle. Now is your chance. But avoid the main road. There is a royal engagement ball in the White Rose Kingdom, Roger said, his voice entering Snow's mind. She tilted her head as she studied the owl for a moment, wondering if she misheard him.

"Who's getting married?" she asked. The

owl shook his feathers like a wet dog and gave a hoot.

The new king is to marry Belle.

Snow's stomach knotted at the mention of the new king. Memories of what she'd done flooded her mind and struck her conscience. Nathaniel could've very well have put her to death, but he showed mercy. As did Belle. But that didn't mean they were still friends.

Snow supposed that Belle might never forgive her for what she'd done. As much as it pained Snow to have lost a good friend, she couldn't blame Belle. It was wrong, and Snow knew it. But Aria needed to be stopped.

Ever since Jack left, she'd been cold and distant. And what she did to George was just the beginning of her evil course. Soon, she made an alliance with Prince John, who was wicked beyond belief. And she took to meddling in other people's affairs. It was like a game of chess to her. People were nothing but pawns, and Snow couldn't just sit back and watch.

She did what she could, but her plan had failed, and now she was locked in a dungeon. Though not for long. Snow looked at the brass key in her hand. Escaping wasn't the problem. Now, finding another way to dethrone her sister, however, *that* was the real challenge.

She had to take another angle. And she couldn't do it alone. The Snow Queen was just too powerful. Snow needed to make allies —strong and powerful allies—which meant... she needed to find a way to get Belle and Nathaniel back on her side.

And there was only one way to achieve that.

She needed to apologize.

Determined, Snow took the brass key and stood. Then she brushed off her damp skirts and rammed the key into the lock.

There are two guards outside the door. I'll distract them, and you'll have a clear path to the stables, Roger said as he took flight.

Snow threw her cloak's hood over her head and carefully opened the metal door. She watched her barn owl fly up the steps and out the open doorway, then heard a shout, followed by a crash.

She smiled. "Good boy, Roger."

She hurried out the door, then scaled the steps, taking two at a time. As she reached the stable, she wasted no time untying Penny, her horse. "Hi there, girl. Are you feeling up for a ride to the White Rose Kingdom?" Snow said, smoothing Penny's mane.

I can't remember the last time we went on a trip, Penny replied with a neigh. Snow fastened the saddle and climbed on.

"Come on, then. Time for an adventure," she whispered in Penny's ear. It flicked back and the horse galloped down the path and into the woods.

A symphony of music flooded the air as Snow and Penny reached the castle. The windows glowed yellow in the night, and a babble of excitable talk greeted them. Guards stood by the front gates, inspecting the line of carriages waiting to enter. Snow set her jaw. There was no way her name would be on the guest list.

She scanned the skies for Roger, but he was nowhere to be seen.

"Stay here," Snow whispered to Penny, not bothering to tether her. She climbed up a tree next to the castle walls and peered over the top. A flood of regal guests filled the castle grounds, and long banquet tables were laden with all manner of fine wines and food. Snow squinted and could just make out Belle in a large, golden gown, standing near the center with Nathaniel, who was wearing crisp, royal attire. They both looked so... formal. It was a far cry from the last time she saw them both, looking disheveled and desperate.

Finally, she spotted Roger flying over the string quartet. She hooted to get his attention, and he changed his direction, landing on her outstretched hand.

Belle is in great distress. Her father is still missing. Nathaniel has had his men searching, Roger said. *Even her brother and his pack haven't been able to track him down.*

Snow frowned. "Crumbs. What do you know about her father?"

He's known to be the greatest inventor in all the land and a collector of rare herbs and artifacts.

"Where do you think a man like that would go?"

I did hear a rumor from the other birds. But I'm

not sure how much truth is in it, Roger offered, ruffling his feathers.

Snow nodded. "Tell me."

Roger twisted his head around and gripped her wrist with his talons. *There's an inventor who has been selling his gadgets on the road. He never stays in the same place for longer than a day. But they saw him yesterday entering Quail Village.*

"That's less than an hour's ride from here," Snow said. A bubble of hope rose to her chest, and she dropped down from the tree.

She mounted Penny, then raced through the forest with Roger flying above their heads until Penny grew tired and they slowed to a canter. Once they reached the village, it was unusually quiet, and the full moon lit up the streets in a silver glow. Snow kept her hood on and jumped down from Penny.

Belle's father should be here, somewhere. Roger's voice entered Snow's mind, but she wasn't entirely sure where he'd landed.

"Go and have a drink," she whispered to Penny, motioning to the water trough outside a tavern. Snow thought about going inside for a drink herself and maybe some food, but it was dark, and she was afraid someone would recognize her. Not so much as the Princess of the Chanted Kingdom, but as The Snow Queen's sister. Aria had made so many enemies, it was no longer safe for Snow to be wandering around the kingdom alone. If anyone knew who she was, she would surely be in trouble.

Instead, she walked the streets, careful to obscure her face with the hood of her cloak whenever she walked by a group of people. She scanned the crooked houses with smoking chimneys, wondering what it would be like to live a common life. A life without having to hide in a wine cellar. Or be imprisoned in a dungeon. Was it too much to ask?

Though even before Aria killed George and The Evil Queen murdered her parents, Snow's life was far from normal. If it weren't for her gift in talking to animals, she wouldn't have been able to survive all the loneliness.

She shook her head, determined not to cry. Now was not the time to get emotional. She was going to find Belle's father and finally reunite him with his daughter, then hopefully gain her support in overthrowing The Snow

Queen. Then she would finally get justice for her beloved George.

A grunt and a thud alerted her to a dark alley to her left. Without hesitation, she ran to the edge of a building and peeked around the corner into the darkness.

A shadowy figure stood near a wagon of hay. When it turned around, the moonlight lit up a pair of brown eyes. Snow released a breath, then stretched her neck to get a better look. The man was older with gray hair, but his narrow nose and scowl reminded her of Belle. She had never met Belle's father before, but the resemblance was unmistakable.

The thrill of finding him before anyone else made her heart skip a beat. She took a step closer but then halted when the moonlight illuminated a glistening, bloody knife in his hand. Snow looked down to see a man dead on the ground, a growing puddle of blood staining the floor.

"I am done being the good one," the killer muttered under his breath.

Snow's heart raced. "Are you... Belle's father?" she asked, her voice shaking as the iron smell of blood filled the alley.

"Not anymore," the man replied, a wicked smile tugging at his lips as he raised the bloody dagger in the air. "Now, I am Rumpelstiltskin."

Snow staggered back a few steps as he stared at her. Then a rush of footsteps approached from behind. Rumpelstiltskin raised a finger to his lips as he wiped the bloody dagger on his clothes. Then he turned away and disappeared into the darkness.

Two men rounded the corner and gasped at the sight of the bleeding man in the alley, their faces turning pale as they looked at Snow in shock. She held up her hood, hiding her face. "What happened here?" one of the men asked. "Who did this?"

Snow turned on her heel as two men hurried to the fallen man. One of them stooped down to check for a pulse. Snow couldn't speak as she continued to back away with a hand over her mouth in horror. Her brain scrambled to make any sense of what she'd just witnessed.

"Wait a minute!" One of the men called out to her. "My lady, did you see who did this?"

Trembling, Snow shook her head. "No, I—I didn't see a thing." Then she turned and ran away before the men could ask any more questions.

Snow couldn't fathom what Belle's father had done. Or what he'd meant by calling himself Rumpelstiltskin. Snow had always heard good things about Belle's father.

But now was not the time to dwell on it. The night was drawing on and Snow couldn't go back to the castle, knowing she wasn't welcome with Belle. There was only one person left she could go to for help.

It was time to pay a certain dwarf a visit.

CHAPTER TWO

A ria adjusted the collar of her gown as she took long strides toward her study. She pushed open the double doors, and the morning light illuminated the room while the spring breeze came from the opened patio. Once inside, she closed the doors, bolting them with a click.

Aria stopped in front of a full-body mirror that hung on the wall. The Mirror of Reason. "Mirror, mirror on the wall..." she said, her cold expression staring back at her. "Show me Snow White."

Her reflection vanished as if the mirror had steamed and fogged up. Then a blurred image of her sister appeared, dismounting from her horse in a village surrounded by construction. Aria peered into the mirror and noticed the small-sized people walking in the background. But it wasn't until she noticed the axe propped on their shoulders that she realized where Snow had run away to.

"The dwarfs' village," Aria muttered. "How predictable." She waved a finger in the air, and the image of her sister vanished. She then turned on her heels and went to stand by the window.

Birds of spring sang outside, but it did nothing to lift her mood. In fact, the noise made her head hurt. Being a villain was a full-time job—and mentally exhausting. She shut her eyes and rubbed her temples. It was hard to remember the last time she had a proper night's sleep.

Actually, that wasn't true. She knew exactly when she'd stopped sleeping. It was the night Jack left her. The memories rushed back despite her best efforts to keep them locked away.

"Aria! Aria, don't walk away from me. What on Earth was that?" Jack said, following Aria as she marched into the castle whilst chaos ensued outside.

Aria walked into her room with Jack close behind. He slammed the door shut. "Talk to me," he demanded, grasping her arms. But Aria couldn't look into his piercing eyes. Jack was so full of goodness. He would never understand.

"I did what I had to," she said, repeating what Grandfather had told her.

"What about George?"

"He was not Snow's true love."

Jack dragged a hand through his white hair. "So... you killed him?"

Aria looked at him finally. "I didn't kill him. You know what the lake is, I just sent him away."

Jack looked at her incredulously. "So, you banished him, then? In front of the whole kingdom? Aria, everyone thinks——"

"That was the whole point, Jack," Aria interrupted. "Everyone thinks I'm a villain. Now, I can fulfill my role."

Jack took her hand. "You don't have to do this. What my grandfather told you... it's not the only way."

Aria shook her head. "They need a villain, Jack. And we killed The Evil Queen. What other choice do I have?"

Jack dropped her hand and cupped her face with

his hands, grazing her bottom lip with his thumb. "You can choose to be good."

He leaned in and brushed his lips over hers. When he pulled away slightly, a light dusting of snow fell around them. Aria's lips twitched as she looked up at the falling snowflakes. Jack tilted his head and looked at her.

"Aria, please," he pleaded. "Let me help you find a better way. We can still help them. Together."

She pulled away with a frown. "No."

The snow evaporated, and Jack frowned at her. He scratched the back of his neck and looked down with his brows knitted together. "I can't stand by and watch you do this."

His words stung. "What is that supposed to mean?"

He gave her one last look before tearing his gaze away. As he turned, Aria grabbed his arm. "You can't leave me."

"No, Aria." He gently removed her hand from him and pulled away. "I can't stay."

Aria opened her eyes and stared out the window, overlooking the Chanted Forest, the same way she had the day she'd watched Jack leaving on his horse. She bit her lip until it stung, surprised the memory still haunted her.

"Mirror, mirror..." she said in a tired voice. "Show me Grandfather."

She turned once more to her own reflection, then it fizzled away and an old man with white hair appeared in its place. He was sitting at a desk, reading with his small round glasses perched on the edge of his nose.

She looked toward his door, wondering if Little Jack would appear like he did last time. She had been communicating with the old man for a while now, but she still couldn't wrap her mind around the time jump between them. Every time she connected with the old man through the mirror, she never knew at what timeline she would catch him. The last time she spoke to him, Jack was a toddler. She got to see him for a fraction of a second when he barged through the door without knocking. If her heart hadn't been so scarred and callous, the mere sight of him would've broken her.

"Aria..." Grandfather looked up from his book and removed his glasses. "Pleasure to see you."

"I wish I could say the same," she replied, walking away from the mirror. She couldn't stand looking at the old man. His facial features, though worn and weathered, resembled Jack too much. It wasn't surprising considering he was his grandson, but seeing his face reminded her of all she'd given up with an uncomfortable jolt.

"What can I do for you?" he asked.

"I need to know what comes next," she said as she took a seat in one of the plush armchairs. She picked up a book and ran her finger along the spine, deep in thought. "I'm going through a lot at the moment, and I can use a distraction."

"Whatever do you mean?" the man in the mirror asked in a level tone. Aria gave him a hard look.

"Don't patronize me, old man. You know exactly what I mean." She flicked back her blonde locks and clamped her teeth against the uncomfortable knot in her stomach.

Since she became The Snow Queen, she had hurt so many people who had once been dear to her.

"Have you already forgotten?" Grandfather asked, placing a bookmark inside his book and shutting it. "Because of you, Red,

Robin, and Belle have all found their happy endings."

"But they all hate me now," Aria said, seething. "Jack left, and my own sister tried to kill me." Aria lifted her hand and stared at the genie bracelet her sister had locked onto her, inhibiting her ice powers. "Who was the idiot who wrote such a miserable fate for The Snow Queen, anyway? He deserves to have his heart ripped out of his chest."

The old man leaned back on his chair and wiped his glasses with a cloth. "Aria, my dear. I know it's hard."

"You know nothing." Aria slammed a fist on a side table. Had she been free from the genie bracelet, it would have turned into a block of ice. "Maybe Jack was right." She rose to her feet. "This was a huge mistake." But it was also too late to rectify. The mess she had gotten herself into was possibly beyond repair, and the only person who could help her rebuild the bridges she had burned was Jack.

"If you want to see Jack, all you have to do is ask the mirror," the old man said calmly. "You know that."

Aria looked toward the window, remembering the last time she'd asked the mirror to show her Jack. She saw a snowy hilltop with huts scattered across it. In the center was a campfire. Jack stood among a group of people, waving his hands, forming a large snowball in thin air. Aria was impressed. His powers were already growing stronger.

She remembered reaching out, but her fingers only touched glass. She whispered his name, but it sounded different on her lips. Distant. Cold. The absence of him made her feel empty. That was the last time she had seen Jack.

She gulped air like a fish out of water and turned to look at Grandfather again. "So, do you have a distraction for me, or not?"

"I might have just what you need," the old man said, his voice surprisingly eager considering Aria's emotionless state.

"Do tell," Aria said, drawing closer to the mirror.

The old man smiled slightly. "It's time for Snow White to find her happy ending."

CHAPTER THREE

*E*mmett held his breath and closed one eye to perfect his aim. His arrow was ready to strike the wolf drinking water from the lake. One kill shot to the heart or to the head and the animal would fall limp to the ground. Why couldn't he just release the arrow?

His brother's gentle voice surfaced from the back of Emmett's mind, pleading for the animal's life. Emmett clenched his jaw, angry at the thought of his brother defending those savages.

But Emmett didn't care. He wasn't like his brother. He hated those creatures. And he would keep hating them for as long as he lived. They killed his parents, and for that alone, he would never stop hunting them down.

The wolf turned his head as if picking up a sound in the distance, and Emmett got a perfect view of his neck. It would be instant death. He drew back the arrow with renewed determination.

Wolves are human too, Emmett. His brother's voice returned. *They have families. Wives... kids. They are someone's parents too.*

Emmett lowered his bow with a frustrated grunt. The wolf turned in his direction. Their eyes locked for a brief moment. Its amber eyes glinted in the weak sunlight, and its ears twitched. Emmett saw nothing human in those eyes. The wolf took off running in the opposite direction, disappearing into the woods with a howl.

Emmett returned the arrow to his quiver, a mixture of anger and shame rising inside of him.

He should hate his brother for having taken the kingdom from him and driven him away. If Nathaniel hadn't chosen the wolves over his own flesh and blood, they could have ruled together, side by side, just like their father wanted. But no. He chose those savages over him, and nothing had ever hurt Emmett more deeply.

A strange ache rippled through him, and he clenched his jaw, pushing away all thoughts of his brother. But it was hard to erase him from his life when the entire kingdom buzzed with the royal wedding approaching. A month had passed since the engagement ball, which meant the wedding was any day now.

Emmett rose to his feet and made his way toward the lake. He crouched by the water but then stopped when he saw his reflection. Even though he'd grown a beard, it was still his twin brother's face that stared back at him. The piercing blue eyes more than anything.

He slapped the water, then scooped up a handful of mud from the edge of the lake. He slid two fingers on both cheeks, making a streak of mud under his eyes. By the time the water stilled enough for him to see his bearded reflection again, the clean-shaven face that resembled his brother was gone. And hopefully, the sting of betrayal would fade soon enough.

Emmett took his bow and arrow, secured his silver sword, and started down the dusty road toward the tavern, where Knight, his horse, was waiting for him.

Knight was his only companion, and a worthy one at that. He didn't complain or shoot him judgmental looks like humans did. But the most valuable aid was that wolves weren't threatened by horses, and the sound of his hooves on the ground helped to mask Emmett's breathing and heartbeat.

The sound of a small cavalry came from behind Emmett, but he didn't bother turning around. Four royal guards with a carriage rode past him, then stopped a few feet ahead as if waiting for Emmett to approach.

"We're looking for a hunter named Emmett," one of the guards said.

Emmett studied them for a moment. They weren't from his kingdom. Their armor was silver and white. "Who's asking?"

"The Snow Queen," the guard said. "She has requested your presence."

"Look, it's hot, I'm hungry, and quite honestly, not in the mood to deal with drama right now." When Emmett took a step forward, all four guards drew their swords and aimed them in his direction.

"She wasn't asking," the guard added.

Emmett gave them a tired look. Could he take on four men? Probably. But like he'd said, he wasn't in the mood for drama. "Fine. But there better be food."

---

*E*mmett entered The Snow Queen's white castle with a guard at each side. He didn't need to be held. He followed them willingly down the large, empty corridors.

From what Emmett had heard, he'd expected the palace to have been made of ice with snow ogres as guards. But the dark wood floors reminded him a lot of his father's study. After he died, however, his study became just another vacant room in the castle. It started to smell like an old lake. The Snow Queen's castle didn't smell much different. He glanced at the rooms as they passed by and noted how still and quiet it was. Their footsteps echoed like beating drums, and Emmett frowned.

The Snow Queen's castle was deserted. Lonely.

The guards stopped in front of an oak door with elaborate markings shaped into a snowflake etched into it, and Emmett braced himself. What did The Queen want with him? He wasn't a king anymore. What could he possibly have that would interest her?

The door opened and the guards guided Emmett inside. Across the room, the Queen sat majestically on her throne wearing a pale blue gown, her white-blonde hair falling in soft waves past her shoulders. At a glance, she was radiant and lovely, hardly having a care in the world. However, the hollowness in her eyes and the permanent line between her brows told him another story. It seemed like she hadn't slept for days. Emmett knew what that felt like. Maybe that was why she summoned him. After all, misery loved company.

Emmett took a step forward, but one of the guards blocked him with a sword, shooting him a dark stare before he looked at the Queen, waiting for her command.

"You may approach," The Snow Queen finally said.

The guards bowed their heads. "As you wish, Your Highness."

Once they approached the white marble throne, they bowed their heads again and took their posts by the door, leaving Emmett by himself in front of the throne. He didn't like standing there on his own, but at least they hadn't taken his weapons. That made him feel just a tad bit more confident in case anything went wrong.

She looked at him from head to toe like he was a painting that didn't impress her. Emmett wasn't offended, but he didn't come all this way to be told something he already knew.

"So, My Queen," Emmett said with an edge in his tone. "Are you going to tell me why I'm here, or will I have to guess?"

"It's Aria," she said, leaning forward. "And I need your sword."

"My sword?" He arched a brow. "Don't your men have swords?"

"Not the silver blade," she replied, lifting her wrist to expose one shiny genie bracelet. "Elven metal isn't easily cut, and your sword is made of the same metal, is it not?"

Emmett pulled his sword from his sheath,

causing the guards to draw their weapons and rush toward him.

"Halt," Aria commanded, raising a hand to stop them. "It's all right." She stood and made her way toward Emmett, stretching out her hand. "May I?"

Emmett hesitated, but only for a moment. He turned the sword around and offered her the handle. Aria took it and, without wasting any more time, she cut herself free from the bracelet, letting it fall to the tile floor with a clang.

She let out a relieved breath as she lifted her hand, an icy mist hovering above her palm.

"What a shame, it looked nice," Emmett muttered, sarcasm evident in his tone.

"Sadly, it can't be destroyed," she replied, handing his sword back. "Thank you for the blade."

When Aria said nothing else but kept watching Emmett, he narrowed his eyes at her.

"Why do I get the feeling there's more?" he said, sheathing his sword.

"Observant," Aria said as if she was checking it off a mental list. "Not bad."

"How may I possibly be of assistance to The Snow Queen?"

"I would like to hire you," she said.

Emmett let out a light chuckle. "Forgive me, but I'm positive you're able to find a perfectly good hunter within your kingdom to catch a wolf for you."

"It's not a wolf I want to catch," Aria said, giving him a serious look. "It's a young woman with *lips red as the rose, hair black as ebony, skin white as snow.*"

Emmett arched a brow. "Why not just sketch her image and post *Wanted* signs all over the kingdom?"

Aria shook her head. "I don't want my enemies to know my sister is out there, defenseless."

Emmett's eyes widened. "Someone took the princess?" His sister was also a princess, and if anyone took her, he would call down fire from heaven until every soul responsible vanished from existence.

"No one took my sister," Aria assured him. "She ran away. But as I'm sure you are already aware, I have many enemies that will gladly take her into captivity. She is not safe out there. Now, what do you say… will you help me or not?"

"What makes you think I'm the best man for this job?"

"Because not only are you skilled with a sword, but you know how to respect a lady."

"So, throwing the sassy princess over my shoulder and bringing her back home, kicking and screaming, is out of the question?"

Aria gave him a pointed look. "She is not sassy. She is sweet and kind, and you will do no such thing," Aria said, pointing a finger at him. "Should you choose to accept my offer, there will be very specific instructions to follow."

Emmett shifted his weight from one foot to the other. "You haven't made me an offer."

"Very well…" Aria smiled, starting to walk circles around him. "I can make you king once more."

"I am not interested in dethroning my brother."

"Good grief, no. Your brother is ten times the king you ever were."

Emmett rolled his eyes. "Duly noted."

"I'm talking about Prince John's throne," Aria added. "With him gone and King Richard sick, there are ways to make you rise again."

Emmett narrowed his eyes. "How is that possible?"

Aria smiled. "I have my ways."

Emmett shook his head. "It doesn't matter. I am not interested in being king. Those days are over for me."

"Very well…" Aria stopped circling and looked at him. She furrowed her delicate brows in thought, tapping a finger to her lips. "Then what's your price? Name it, and it is yours."

Emmett thought about it for a long moment. What did he want?

He wanted to walk away from the past and never look back. But how could he do that when his own reflection reminded him of it all?

Emmett knew Aria was powerful, but even she lacked the ability to make him look like someone else. But perhaps he could go somewhere new. Somewhere people wouldn't know of him or his brother at all. "Safe passage and residence to one of the northern kingdoms," he said. "Past the King of the Shores."

Aria thought about it. "That would not be an easy task. They hate you over there."

"I am aware."

"And no matter how much mud you put on your face, you still look like your brother. There will be no hiding."

Emmett felt a sting in the pit of his stomach. "I am also aware."

"But the King of the Shores will do just about anything for a flipping mermaid," Aria continued as if Emmett had never spoken at all. "I'm sure I can work something out in your favor." She turned to face Emmett with a pleased smile. "Perfect. It's a deal, then."

"Brilliant," Emmett replied with no emotion at all. "I'll start my search right away."

"No need to search," Aria said, making her way back to her throne. "The dwarfs have made a new settlement on the border, west of here. They have Snow in their care."

Emmett arched a brow. "If you know she's

at the new dwarfs' village, why not just send your guards to get her?"

"Because my sister is determined to dethrone me," Aria explained as she took a seat back on her throne. "And she won't stop until she's tried everything."

"So what am I to do, exactly?" Emmett asked. "Change her mind?"

"On the contrary," Aria said. "I want you to help her."

"Help her?" Emmett echoed. "You want me to help her *dethrone* you?"

"Like I said, she's not going to stop until she's tried everything," Aria repeated. "But I'm afraid of her going at it alone. I don't want her to ally herself with the wrong people. She's never lived outside of these walls. I want to make sure she stays safe."

"So, you're asking me to be her personal guard?"

"Yes. And when she fails, bring her home."

Emmett nodded. "May I ask you a question?"

Aria cocked her head curiously, which Emmett took as permission to continue.

"If she's so determined to destroy you... why do you want her back?"

"Because..." Aria narrowed her ice-blue eyes. She seemed surprised at his question, as if the answer was obvious. "You don't give up on family."

Another sharp stab pierced at Emmett's stomach. "Well, if there's nothing else, I'll be on my way."

"Actually, there is one more thing," Aria added, her rosy lips curving up into an amused smile. "Make sure to be... *charming*."

CHAPTER FOUR

*S*now looked out of the little open window as she absent-mindedly rolled out pastry. Roger nestled into a groove in a tree trunk and snoozed the day away. How he could sleep among all the noise, Snow had no idea. But Roger was not like any other barn owl. He was inventive too. She wouldn't have been surprised if he had somehow fashioned earplugs out of mud to block out the sound of the dwarfs working on the new houses.

Since their village was destroyed by The Evil Queen, the dwarfs relocated to the very edge of the Chanted Forest. A river cut through the line of houses and opened out into a vast lake, where all manner of wildlife gathered.

The trees were mature and seemingly untouched by the harsh winters they had been having. Lush green leaves rustled in the soft breeze, and as spring arrived, juicy red berries grew on every tree.

After turning up to their house at an indecent time in the middle of the night, Snow had stayed with the dwarfs. They let her rest on two of their beds pushed together while they slept on the floor in the living room. All they wanted in return was a warm meal at the end of the day and for her to tell them stories at night.

They were out the door by the time the sun rose and worked on building houses until the sun sunk in the horizon. They never stopped to eat or drink. So, Snow was glad to be of assistance.

She soon settled into a routine. When she woke up in the morning, she collected the smelly clothes littered on the floors of the cabin and took them to a large basin outside. She sang with the birds as she scrubbed the clothes clean and hung them out to dry.

After that, she folded the sheets, made the beds, and swept the floors. The hard work reminded her of the years she spent hidden in the cellar after The Evil Queen killed her parents. She didn't particularly enjoy having been hidden in a cellar, but she did enjoy learning to do things for herself.

Snow closed her eyes, smiling sadly to herself. If she ever returned to the palace, she would thank Mara, her maid, for everything she'd done. Now that her plans were foiled again, she wasn't sure when or how she would return to the palace.

Roger kept Snow updated on the whispers in the forest. It was tremendously helpful that birds simply loved to gossip. To the average human, they simply heard tweetings, assuming the birds were singing playful songs, or making the occasional mating call.

But Snow knew better. The tweets often started off with *good heavens, come and listen to this!* Or *You won't guess what I heard on the grapevine this morning!*

The latest gossip was about Nathaniel and Belle's wedding. They had finally picked a date now that her father had been found. No one, however, said anything about Rumpelstiltskin. Snow wondered if they knew what he'd become.

How will that work? a brown bird asked, flapping its wings. *If they have babies, will they be human or a beast?*

Snow snorted as she draped the cut-out pastry over the pie dish, covering up the gooseberries she had foraged the day before.

"Don't think too much, Petri. You'll make yourself dizzy," Snow teased the brown bird, and if a bird could blush, Petri would have.

My head does feel a little funny.

Snow chuckled, then pointed to the pie. "Can I get a little help?" she asked, patting her hands on her apron. Petri whistled and flew in through the window, settling on the edge of the pie. Then he hopped all around the circumference, making a criss-cross pattern in the pastry.

"Thank you," Snow said, beaming at the little bird. She rested her hands on her hips, surveying the small pie for a moment, and frowned. "This won't be enough. I need to make another."

She picked up the cloth bag from the

counter and groaned at the sight of just two lonely gooseberries at the bottom. "I'll need to go out and gather some more," she said to no one in particular.

Snow took off her apron and hung it on a little wooden hook by the door. She then brushed a few stray hairs away from her face and pulled on her ankle boots.

The sun poured in through the trees, touching the forest floor like millions of sparkling diamonds. Snow had never been this far outside the palace walls before.

The animals were friendly, albeit a little nosy, but the people in the dwarf village were so welcoming. As Snow strolled deeper into the woods, swinging her cloth bag as she whistled to the birds, she wondered if she should forget about The Snow Queen altogether and focus on starting a new life, away from the palace.

She welcomed the idea, but a snap under her feet jolted her out of her thoughts and, in one swoop, something wrapped around her ankle and she flew upwards. The world turned upside down as she hung in the air by her foot.

Snow shrieked, wishing she had not opted

to wear a dress that day. She thrashed around the air, trying to push her skirts back over her knees, all while trying to reach the thick rope tied around her ankle.

A small chuckle interrupted her struggle. "Well, you're not a wolf."

Snow stopped wrestling, pinning the skirts to her knees. Her heartbeat throbbed against her temples as she looked around, searching for the man who had spoken.

"I most certainly am not," she said. Finally, her gaze landed on a man with dark hair, his short brown curls oiled to look neat and glossy in the sun.

Snow squinted and tilted her head, also noticing the piercing blue eyes. "King Nathaniel?"

The man frowned for a flicker of a second but then settled back into a casual grin as he leaned against a tree with his arms crossed. "No, my lady. My name is Emmett."

"Oh," Snow said, not sure what else to say. Emmett was Nathaniel's twin brother, and she wasn't sure if he knew what she had done to his brother. If he knew, he would surely keep her tied up forever.

"Hold on, I'll get you down," Emmett said, coming toward her. He took a knife and held it between his teeth as he dragged an arm around Snow's back. The flood of spicy coriander scent brought color to her cheeks. In her mind, being that close to a strange man was scandalous.

He clutched her so tightly that the side of her face pressed against his firm chest, and Snow held her breath. Emmett reached up and began freeing her from the net as she held her skirts over her knees until her hands began to tremble.

Emmett grunted, and the sound rumbled against Snow's ears. She hadn't been that close to a man since... she bit her lip as George's face flashed before her eyes.

"Hold on," Emmett warned. The rope snapped, and Snow yelped as she began to fall.

But then Emmett caught her, securing his grip around her body. "It's all right, I've got you," he murmured into her ear. Slowly, he lowered her to the ground, and Snow's dress fell to her ankles as she stood.

"Thank you," she said, pressing a hand to

her racing heart and cursing it for fluttering like that around anyone other than George.

Now that she was back upright, she could take a proper look at the man who had trapped her.

He flashed her a charming smile as he sheathed his knife. Muscles bulged from his ivory cotton shirt, and he had an axe strapped to his back in a leather holder. He was definitely not Nathaniel. Emmett looked more like a hunter than a king.

Snow smiled bashfully as she tucked a strand of hair behind her ear. After a few awkward moments of looking around, she noticed a bird swoop over Emmett's head and begin to tweet.

At least, that was what Emmett was hearing. Instead, Snow heard, *He's so handsome! I can't wait to tell the others about this.*

Snow resisted the urge to laugh as the bird flew away. She focused on Emmett, realizing that he had started talking.

"...once again, I am terribly sorry you got caught in one of my traps."

Snow giggled and waved her hands. "It's no problem. No harm done," she insisted.

"Thank you for rescuing me. I'm not sure how to repay you…" Then Snow was struck by an idea. "Do you like gooseberry pie?"

"I love pie," Emmett said, his face lighting up.

The forest echoed with birds chirping, *He likes pie! He likes pie!*

Snow ignored them. "Then I insist you take a slice with you on your travels," she said, picking up her dress and walking down the path. "Come with me."

Emmett's smile grew wider as he inclined his head. "Well, if you insist, it would be rude for me to decline."

Snow bit against a grin as she led Emmett back to the dwarfs' village.

CHAPTER FIVE

On arriving at the dwarfs' village, it was buzzing with the sound of hard work. Hammers against nails, axes chopping wood, and the smell of melted metal filled the air. The people didn't even seem to notice them walking by. Either that or they were simply very discreet.

"Snow, sweetheart," a dwarf woman with wild curly hair approached them with something in her hand. Emmett stood behind Snow as she crouched to speak to the woman. "Here's the jar for the grape jelly you made for us."

"Was it any good?" Snow asked, her voice sweet and kind, just as Aria had described.

"Oh, it was delightful!" the woman cooed. "And we spread it on the bread just as you said. It was absolutely heavenly, darling. I'll bring you more grapes in a few days."

Snow smiled, taking the empty jar. "That will be lovely, Zinda. Thank you."

Zinda looked up at Emmett, beaming. "And who is this?"

"Oh, this is Emmett," Snow said, stepping aside. "He's..." She paused, then gave him a questioning look. Emmett supposed she knew he'd been royal but didn't seem entirely sure how to introduce him.

"I'm a huntsman," Emmett said, offering Zinda a smile. "Pleased to meet you."

"Oooh, a huntsman." Zinda batted her lashes and fanned herself. "Very good with your hands, I presume."

Snow giggled, and Emmett suppressed a smile.

"I, for one, find a man with an axe irresistible," Zinda added.

"Zinda!" A gruff dwarf with a raspy voice and gray hair stepped outside of a small house. He must've seen Zinda batting her lashes at Emmett because he threw his axe over his shoulder and stomped over to them with a crease formed between his brows. "So, you good with an axe now, ain't you?"

"Oh, Larry." Zinda brushed his shoulder. "Leave the handsome huntsman alone."

"Huntsman, huh?" Larry looked up at Emmett, unimpressed. "What do you hunt?"

"Wolves."

A flicker of surprise crossed Larry's face, but then it vanished as quickly as it came. "Have you heard that White Rose Kingdom has made it illegal to hunt wolves? People are saying The Snow Queen might adopt to the same law."

Emmett nodded. "I've heard rumors."

"That means you will soon be out of a job. How fast can you cut a tree and chop its logs?"

Emmett looked at Snow. Was that a rhetorical question?

Snow smiled. "They have a log-cutting competition every so often," she explained. "Larry here is one of our champions."

"Oh, yes." Zinda leaned on Larry's shoulder. "My Larry is one of the best."

Larry lifted a finger to Emmett. "A man is

not a real man until he's cut a tree's worth of logs."

Emmett nodded. "Duly noted."

"Let me see your axe, son." Larry stretched out his hand. Emmett pulled the axe from his back and handed it to the old dwarf. He examined it for a long moment. "When was the last time you sharpened the blade?"

Emmett wasn't sure. He didn't carry an axe as often as he did his silver sword, or his bow and arrows. "It's been a while," he replied, only to get a bossy glare from Larry.

"You can tell a lot about a man by the way he treats his axe."

Emmett wasn't sure how to respond. Or why his value as a man rested entirely on a rusty axe.

"Come on." Larry turned on his heels and waved at Emmett to follow. "I'll show you the right way to sharpen a blade."

"Larry, that's so kind of you," Snow cut in. "But it's not necessary. We were just about to eat some pie."

Larry gave Snow a fatherly scowl. "Every man earns his pie around here, young lady.

Have we taught you nothing?" He walked away and headed toward his shed.

Snow turned to Emmett with an apologetic look, but he didn't mind. He actually found it quite amusing. "I guess I'll go earn my pie," he teased.

She smiled, two small dimples indenting her cheeks. And for a brief moment he found himself thinking the job wasn't going to be as unbearable as he initially thought.

"Come with me, darling." Zinda reached for Snow's hand and pulled her along. "We need to start dinner. By the time my Larry is done with him, he will be famished."

Snow gave one last glance over her shoulder, the apologetic expression still plastered on her delicate face, then disappeared into Zinda's little crooked house. Emmett's face fell as he watched the creaky front door slam shut.

"Come on, young man!" Larry yelled from the shed. "We ain't got all day."

Emmett squared his shoulders and took a deep breath. He wasn't particularly nervous, but he did feel the strangest desire to impress the man. After all, how hard was it to sharpen an axe?

*E*mmett's muscles throbbed as he chopped yet another log over a tree stump. His cotton shirt was drenched in sweat, and he hadn't been allowed a break for far too long. *Breaks are for the weak,* he kept looping Larry's words in his mind. *Real men tough it out.*

That may have been the motto in the dwarf village, but for Emmett, he was only a few breaths away from passing out and, most certainly, not earning his pie.

The sight of Snow approaching with a cold glass of lemonade was like a mirage in a desert. He dropped the newly sharpened axe on the ground and wiped his brow with his forearm.

"I was starting to think you forgot about me," he said, taking the cold drink.

"I thought he was just going to show you how to sharpen the thing," Snow said, watching Emmett with guilt in her eyes. She clearly regretted leaving him alone.

Emmett nodded but was too busy to reply since he was chugging down the refreshing liquid. When he finished, he wiped his mouth with the back of his hand. "We *started* by sharpening the blade," he said, motioning to the stack of logs next to him. "Then, of course, we had to make sure the axe was sharp enough."

"Okay, I say you've earned your pie, mister," Snow said, reaching for his hand and pulling him along. "Let's go."

"Where?" he asked, though not resisting. The farther away she got him from that pile of logs, the better.

"To my cottage," she said. "You should freshen up before my friends come home."

Snow led the way to a small hut on the edge of the village. It had a thatch roof and a smoking chimney that blew out puffs of cloud into the sky. The hammering wasn't as loud, and the smell of burned coals grew weak, giving way to the delicious scent of sweet berries. When he finally entered the cottage, the inviting smell of gooseberry pie filled his senses, and his stomach grumbled.

"Sorry about the mess," Snow apologized, her cheeks turning pink as she picked up the many pieces of clothing scattered over the home. "Living with seven men is no walk in the park."

"You live with seven men?"

"Dwarfs," she added. "They're Larry and Zinda's kids. Adult kids, actually. Anyway, the bath is in the back."

"Thank you. I just need to get my bag outside." By the time Emmet returned, Snow had prepared his bath with warm water. After stripping off his clothes, he relaxed inside the tin tub. He hadn't taken a warm bath in almost a month, and the heat soothed his screaming shoulders.

He'd been living his life as a nomad, and bathing in lakes and waterfalls had become the norm. It wasn't bad during spring, but he would need to come up with another plan for the winter.

After he ended his bath and drained the water, Emmett changed into fresh clothes and walked out, drying his short brown hair with his hand. He stopped when he saw Snow across the room with her back to him. She had perfect posture, and the ties of her apron fastened into a white bow at her tiny waist. She stood behind the stove, stirring a large pot.

"He's just a friend," Snow muttered. "Now, quit it or you're not getting any pie."

Emmett looked around the room, wondering who she was talking to. He noticed a squirrel standing upright on the window's ledge. He lifted his tiny arms in the air, then let out a series of high pitch squeaks.

Snow shook her head with a giggle. "I'm not listening."

Emmett chuckled. The only other woman he'd ever seen talking to animals was his mother while she was gardening. She would also talk to the plants and the flowers too. According to her, they were all living things and needed attention. Emmet found himself smiling at the pleasant memory. Those didn't often come into his mind, so it was refreshing.

"All done," he said, pretending to have just walked out.

"Feeling better?" Snow asked, looking over her shoulder, her black hair still obscured half of her face, so all that Emmett could see was a pair of pouty red lips and a soft button nose.

"My muscles are going to be sore for a few days," he confessed, joining her in the kitchen, which was a small space in the corner of the living room. "But the bath was great. Thank you."

Snow smiled. "You're welcome."

"Hey, Princess—" A group of dwarfs walked into the home, then stopped by the door as soon as they spotted Emmett standing next to Snow.

"Snow." An angry dwarf stepped in front of the group and crossed his arms. "What is that giant doing in our home?"

Snow gave him a *be polite* look. "He's not a giant, he's a family friend. Now, go clean up. Supper is ready," she said, putting out the fire from underneath the large pot.

"Do I smell pie?" a dwarf with big ears and playful eyes asked, leaning over the island counter with his tongue sticking out like a dopey dog. "Is it gooseberry pie? Oh, let it be gooseberry pie!" He swooned his head as if already imagining what that first bite would taste like.

A loud sneeze came from behind Emmett, making him jump. A dwarf with a red nose and puffy eyes smiled up at him. "Sorry, it's hay fever season and I have bad allergies," he said in a stuffy voice.

"You're tall," a dwarf with round glasses said, squinting up at Emmett. "Did you know that if you go very high up, the elevation will make your nose bleed? Have you ever gotten a nosebleed?"

Emmett shook his head. "Only from a fight."

"A fight?" another dwarf said, yawning from across the room. "Why would anyone want to exert energy on a fight?"

"Will he be staying for supper?" another dwarf whispered bashfully to Snow. When Emmett glanced at him, he hid behind her.

"Enough stalling," Snow announced. "Now, go clean up before sitting at the table."

As the little men made their way to the back of the cottage, she proceeded to pour the vegetable stew into a bowl.

"Would you mind putting this on the table, please?"

"Sure." Emmett was about to grab the bowl when the angry dwarf jumped between them.

"I'll get it," he said, glaring at Emmett

before taking the bowl and walking across the room to place it on the table with a thud.

Emmett leaned his back against the counter next to Snow and crossed his arms, watching as the angry dwarf came back for six more bowls.

Snow poured another two bowls of stew, then covered the pot. "Here you go," she handed Emmett one of the bowls and a spoon, then turned toward the door. "Follow me."

Outside, a thick log sat sideways, surrounded by a group of cherry trees, their pink and white blossoms in full bloom. Snow took a seat, and Emmett settled next to her. They ate in silence as the evening sky began to sparkle with stars and petals floated to the ground like feathers. When it grew too dark to see, Emmett made a fire in front of them, then returned to sit next to her.

"The food was delicious," he said above the crackling of the fire. "Where did you learn to cook like that?"

Snow arched a brow. "Why is it surprising that I know how to cook?"

Emmett offered her a small smile,

wondering what to tell her, but Snow seemed to read his thoughts as though they were written all over his face.

"You heard them call me 'Princess,' didn't you?"

Emmett shrugged. "Not if you didn't want me to."

Snow peered into the fire for a long moment. "Zinda," Snow said. "After The Evil Queen killed my parents, Larry and Zinda, who used to work at the castle, hid me in a little cellar in the garden. She used to come often to check on me, but in the event that she no longer could, she taught me how to cook so I could look after myself."

"That was nice of them," Emmett said.

Snow nodded. "They saved my life."

When Emmett said nothing else, Snow looked at him. The reflection of the fire danced in her eyes. "What about you?" she asked. "What's a king doing wandering about in the wild?"

Emmett let out a long breath. "Well, let's see. I had a misunderstanding with my brother and gave up the throne. Sounds somewhat foolish saying it aloud, but trust me, it needed to be done."

"It doesn't sound foolish at all," Snow replied. "In fact, it makes perfect sense. You're a wolf hunter, and he's a..."

When Snow turned away to look into the fire again, Emmett caught her frowning. "You know what my brother is?"

Snow didn't answer for several heartbeats, then she turned and gave him a small smile, her pretty eyes twinkling like stars. "Not if you don't want me to."

Emmett chuckled. "Fair enough. So, how come you know my brother, but we've never met?"

Snow shook her head. "I don't really know your brother. My sister, *The Snow Queen*, was good friends with Belle. And she's his bride now, so… I just mostly heard of him."

"Your sister is The Snow Queen?" he asked, pretending to be surprised. Thankfully, she didn't notice anything out of the ordinary. Though her smile evaporated, and the corners of her mouth tugged downward.

"Sadly, yes."

"From what I hear, she doesn't have the best reputation."

Snow let out a chuckle. "Now, that's the understatement of the century."

"Take it from me. When a leader makes that many enemies... it's only a matter of time before they're brought to their knees."

"I don't know," Snow muttered under her breath, still watching the fire dance in front of them. "She's too powerful."

"You can be just as powerful," he assured her.

Snow laughed. "Yeah, right."

"I'm serious." When Snow shook her head, Emmett turned his body to face her. "Snow, look at me." He waited, and when she did, he held her gaze. "I have killed more wolves than I can count. But that wasn't because I was stronger than them. It was because I learned to be smart with a weapon."

Snow stared at him with eyes unblinking.

"Now, if you want..." he said, cocking his head. "I can teach you."

"You would do that?" she asked, surprised.

"I think every woman should learn to

defend herself," he said. "That's why I taught my sister to fight."

"Marian knows how to fight?" Snow echoed.

"She may have chosen to be a healer," he said with a shrug. "But give her a sword, and she becomes someone else entirely."

Snow smiled, her face beaming. "And you can teach me that?"

A smug smile tugged at Emmett's lips as he leaned into her. "How does first thing in the morning sound?"

CHAPTER SIX

Snow woke up early the next day to get through her chores before Emmett got up. She was giddy at the idea of learning how to fight.

All her life she had to be protected. When The Evil Queen killed her parents and Aria ran off into the forest, Snow was hidden away like a delicate vessel. She would've loved to learn to fight, but George refused to teach her. He insisted that he would always be there to protect her. His voice was still in her head.

My sweet, delicate Snowflake. So kind and innocent. I want to wrap you up in cotton and hide you from this wicked world.

But now he was gone, and she had no

choice but to fend for herself. She gritted her
teeth and scrubbed the last dish a little harder
than usual as the memory sliced through her
heart like a hot knife.

The dwarfs were in a particularly dim
mood as they shuffled out the front door,
grumbling to each other, though Snow
couldn't work out why. She shook away the
thought and waved at them from the window.
Roger hooted and landed on her shoulder.

They don't like the strange man.

Snow opened her mouth with surprise.
"Emmett? Why not?"

They think he's hiding something, Roger hooted
back.

Snow frowned. "Aren't we all?"

*It's just that he doesn't have the most charming
reputation, but you already know that.* Roger
yawned, then ruffled his feathers. *Now, whistle
if you need me.* Without any further thought, he
flew to his favorite tree and settled under a
shady spot.

"The dwarfs have reason to be cynical,"
Snow thought aloud. "Humans haven't treated
them well in the past." She remembered
seeing the smoke from their village that rose

into the air for weeks after The Evil Queen burned it down in a fit of rage.

All because she was trying to force Aria out of hiding.

Snow set her jaw. Aria had always been the cause of all her problems. Even before she became the formidable Snow Queen, she was getting people killed.

With renewed determination, Snow dried her hands on her apron and set it on the counter. She looked down at her brown pants and remembered how it used to be a dress. Living in a village that was always under construction didn't seem practical not to have pants, and since no one in the village was the same size as her, she got to practice her sewing skills quite a bit. She had sewn herself many clothes during her time in hiding, becoming quite quick with a needle. A knock on the door snapped her from her thoughts. Emmett peeked his head inside.

"Perfect timing," she said with a lopsided grin, reaching for her cloak.

His gaze scanned her body until his piercing eyes met hers again. Something quivered inside Snow's midriff.

"Are you ready, Princess?" he asked with an expectant smile.

Snow pulled her ebony black hair into a bun, then joined him outside, shutting the door behind her. "As ready as I'll ever be."

---

*E*mmett took Snow deep into the woods, and by the time they stopped in a clearing, she was out of breath. The sun beat down on her cheeks, and the pollen in the air clung to the back of her throat, making her cough.

"This is perfect. We'll train here," Emmett said, handing her a sheepskin bag. "Replenish your fluids. You'll need them." He winked, then removed this heavy satchel from his shoulder and dropped it with a clunk to the ground.

Snow took greedy gulps of the tepid water, closing her eyes as the sun warmed her face. Suddenly, a flock of birds giggled overhead, and Snow opened her eyes to find out what was so funny.

Her gaze landed on Emmett as he pulled

his shirt over his head, his back rippling with muscles, shining with sweat.

He turned, and Snow got an eyeful of his beautifully sculpted pectorals. When he caught her watching, she averted her eyes, her cheeks flushing so hard, she wasn't sure where to look.

"All right, take off your cloak and lay it on the ground," Emmett instructed. Snow couldn't stop her mouth from hanging open. The sound of the birds' laughter had her heart thumping.

"Excuse me! I'll have you know I'm a lady," she said, resting her hands on her hips but still unable to look at the half-naked man standing before her.

He howled with laughter, and it broke her out of her embarrassed state. "Before any physical exertion, stretching is important."

"Oh." Snow gawped like a fish as she shakily removed her cloak, letting it fall like a waterfall to the ground. "Right."

Emmett leaned over and touched his toes, urging Snow to do the same. After stretching for a bit, he laid on his back and tapped on the space next to him. When Snow didn't move, he chuckled.

"Have you never done sit-ups before?" he asked. "How else are we going to strengthen your core? Now, watch what I do and try to do the same."

Snow nodded, keeping her eyes on his chiseled abs as he demonstrated, his muscles going taut as he pulled up his upper body.

"Come on, your turn."

Snow shook her head, trying to focus as she settled next to him. She followed his exact movements, but within seconds, she throbbed and ached.

"This is payback for what Larry put you through yesterday, isn't it?" she said between heavy breaths.

"You've done five sit-ups," Emmett said, amused. The glistening sweat on his body sizzled, and Snow's mouth grew dry as she watched him.

"You need to be strong and agile to fight," he said, apparently oblivious to Snow's impure thoughts.

"Right," she said, refocusing. "What's next?"

Emmett's grin grew wider. "Have you ever shot an arrow?"

---

*B*eads of sweat clung to Snow's temples as she stood still with a heavy bow outstretched. She nocked an arrow like Emmett taught her and took a low steady breath.

"Great, that's it. Now, pull back and let go, nice and steady now," Emmett said, his voice low but authoritative.

Run away! A hunter is trying to kill us all!

Snow tried to ignore the squirrel scurrying through the trees and focused on the target. A tree trunk across the clearing with a carved circle on it. Shutting one eye and aiming the arrow at the bullseye, she drew it back and released.

The arrow caught a breeze and changed direction midair, landing on a tree stump instead. Snow lowered the bow with a frustrated huff.

Emmett chuckled as he stood up behind her. "You're doing great. Come on, try again," he said, his body pressing up against her back. He brought his solid arms around Snow's body, wrapping her up in his strength and overwhelming her senses with his earthy scent.

His hot breath tickled her ear as he whispered, "Take the arrow, and aim it at the bullseye…" He found her hands and helped her raise the bow once more. She took shallow breaths, and her mind grew dizzy, overstimulated by Emmett's touch, her aching limbs, and the anxious wildlife all around her.

"Okay, I can do this," she whispered. Emmett let go of her and stepped back. Suddenly, Snow had a chill in the absence of his heat. Still, she aimed at the target again and pulled back the arrow.

A twig snapped to her left and she let go of the arrow with a yelp. The arrow sailed through the air, missing the target and disappearing deep into the forest. A whimpering howl followed, and Snow looked at Emmett in horror. "I hit something." Her face fell with her bow.

Emmett's eyes glinted as he grinned at her. "I dare say you're right. Well done. Let's go and see."

Snow grabbed her cloak, trembling from head to toe, and followed Emmett through the trees. When they reached a small wolf writhing on the ground and making high-pitched yelps, Snow sank to her knees with a bubble of emotion rising up her throat and threatening to fall in giant tears.

"It's a wolf," Emmett said with a mixture of surprise and delight. He unsheathed his silver knife and marched forward. Snow screeched and scrambled to the wolf before he could get to him.

"No! You can't kill him!" She lifted her hands. "He's just a boy."

Emmett looked at her quizzically, lifting a dark brow. "A boy?"

Snow rested a hand on the wolf's leg that had been struck by her arrow. Luckily, the arrow only grazed it, but dark drops of blood began to weep out of the wound. Snow draped her cloak over the wolf's body and bowed her head.

"Show him who you are."

He'll hurt me. He's a hunter.

"He won't hurt you, trust me," she whispered, staring into the gray eyes.

Promise?

"I promise."

"Are you talking to it?" Emmett asked. But then he gasped as the wolf transformed into a young boy with a mop of blond hair. Snow ripped the bottom of her cloak and tied it around the boy's leg, then applied pressure on it.

She looked up at Emmett, who stood frozen on the spot, the silver knife still in his hand.

"See?" She offered him a smile. "Just a boy."

Emmett sheathed his knife and rubbed the back of his neck. He didn't seem one bit comfortable with that revelation. "So, now what?" he asked, his voice torn.

Snow looked back at the young boy. He was panting, and his eyes were wide with fear. She looked back at Emmett. "We need to take him back to the village."

"Doesn't he need a healer?" Emmett asked.

"It's *illegal* to hunt wolves, Emmett," Snow reminded him. "So, unless you know a healer we can trust, we could be thrown in jail for this."

Emmett was silent for a long moment, but then his eyes met hers. "I do."

Snow gave him a quizzical look. "You do… what?"

"I know a healer we can trust."

CHAPTER SEVEN

*A*ria watched as Emmett picked up the boy from the ground and carried him through the forest.

"Enough." She waved a hand over the mirror and the image vanished. Rubbing her tired eyes, she paced back and forth. "Why can't he just kiss her already and live happily ever after?"

"I don't think that's how it works, my dear," a man's voice came from her patio, and Aria swung around. An older man with white hair and wrinkles on the edge of his eyes stood there, leaning against the open glass door.

"Who're you?" she asked, lifting a hand, ready to strike if necessary.

"I'm Rumpelstiltskin," he said, bowing his head respectfully. "But you can call me Rumpel. After all, you and I can make a powerful alliance."

Aria crossed her arms. "And why would I make an alliance with you?"

Rumpel smiled. "Because the alternative is animosity, and you don't strike me as a woman who makes bad decisions."

Aria couldn't help but laugh. "Clearly, you know *nothing* about me."

"Perhaps not…" He entered the room and took a seat on the sofa, crossing his legs. "But I do know you have a mirror that shows you anything you want."

Aria leaned against the back of a chair. "And?"

"And I'm looking to find something," he said vaguely. "I was hoping you could ask your mirror to locate it for me." Before Aria could even think to refuse, he raised a hand. "I'll make you a deal."

Aria narrowed her eyes. "What kind of deal?"

Rumpel pulled out a parchment from his pocket and held it up. "Safe passage to the

Northern Realm. Isn't that what you promised the huntsman if he brought your sister home safely?"

Aria's eyes widened, and she moved away from him. "How do you know about that?"

Rumpel smiled. "You really shouldn't make promises you can't keep, my queen."

"I was going to figure something out."

He cocked his head, amused. "You and I both know those sailors would rather face The Evil Queen ten times over than have any dealings with you. The harsh winter really put a *damper* on their work."

Aria pinched the bridge of her nose. "How many times will I have to say it?" she hissed. "The harsh winter was not. My. Fault."

"Downside of being The Snow Queen," Rumpel said callously. "Now, back to business, shall we?" He lifted the parchment and waved it in the air. "Do we have a deal?"

Aria squared her shoulders and gave him a hard look. "What do you want me to find?"

Rumpel flashed a wide grin. "A special gift for my daughter's wedding."

CHAPTER EIGHT

*E*ven as a king, Emmett was never one to care much about luxury. But on crossing into Sherwood territory while riding on a wooden wagon, he really missed the smooth roads of his kingdom. Holes the size of craters made the wagon ride a lot more unpleasant. It didn't help that the wound on the child's leg was turning purple, increasing the sense of urgency. Emmett had no idea what that meant, but he knew it wasn't good. And the uneven terrain made it that much harder to pick up the pace. Good thing Snow knew the conditions of the road ahead of time because she made sure to add lots of pillows and blankets so the boy wouldn't be hitting against the hard wood.

"He's asleep," Snow said, climbing over the wooden seat to settle next to Emmett as he held the reins of his horse. The dwarfs had offered their horse to go with their wagon, but leaving Knight behind wasn't even an option.

"We already crossed into Sherwood," Emmett said. "We should be arriving at the village soon."

"Thank you for doing this," Snow said, her voice soft as the evening sky sparkled with stars. "I know it couldn't have been easy for you."

He knew what she meant. He walked away from his brother because of his allegiance to wolves, but yet, here he was, helping one. The irony of it all surprised even him, but he wasn't doing it for the creature. He was doing it for the child. And even though Snow thought they were one and the same, that wasn't true. Not to Emmett.

"Back in the woods," he finally spoke. "You had a conversation with the boy before he shifted. How did you do that?"

Snow watched Emmett for a moment,

knowing he never acknowledged her last statement. Thankfully, she didn't press him because talking about his family wasn't a pleasant topic for him.

"I don't just talk to animals," Snow said, shifting her attention to the darkening road ahead. "I can hear them speak. In my head."

Emmett gave her a sideways glance, but she kept her gaze forward. Whether she was embarrassed about her special ability or not, he couldn't tell.

"To others, it just sounds like they're squeaking or quacking," she went on. "But to me, I hear them just as clearly as a human."

"What do they say?" Emmett asked, intrigued.

"Oh, all sorts of things." She chuckled as if remembering something in particular. "I can't speak for all birds, but the ones in the Chanted Forest are known for their gossip. Roger, on the other hand, is not only great at keeping a lookout for danger, but he's quite the collector."

Emmett raised a brow. "Who's Roger?"

"My barn owl," she said, pointing her thumb to the back of the wagon. Emmett was tempted to glance back. He had no idea they had an owl riding with them. "I've had him since I was little. He was the size of the palm of my hand. I was playing in the garden with my sister when she blasted a dagger of ice by mistake, and it hit the top of a tree. An owl's nest fell on the ground, and there he was, with these big black eyes staring up at me." Snow smiled at the memory. "He was trembling, so I picked him up and asked him if he was okay. That's when I heard him speak for the very first time."

When Snow's smile faded, Emmett could tell her first experience must've really scared her.

"What did he say?" Emmett asked.

"He asked me if I was going to hurt him," Snow replied. "I was so scared, I dropped him back on the grass and ran inside." She paused as if trying to remember what followed. "I spent the rest of the day in my room, shoving my head under a pillow, trying to block out the sound of him calling for his mama and papa. He was so scared. And I thought for sure I was going out of my mind. Especially when I told my sister, and still, she could only hear him *hoot*."

"So, what did you do?"

"My sister assured me that there was nothing wrong with me. Maybe I was special like she was, and I should embrace my gift. Then, that same night after supper, she came into my room and handed me a box. When I opened it, the baby owl was inside. She told me it was going to be our little secret. So, I kept him in my room, and we talked every day for hours on end. Oh, and he was jealous of my sister."

"The owl was *jealous*?" Emmett echoed.

"Well, he also hated that Aria kept calling him *fuzzy chick*." Snow laughed, and Emmett found himself uplifted by the joyful sound. "I never told him that, but he really did look like a fuzzy little chick when we found him." Snow paused for a moment, then giggled. "Sorry."

Emmett gave her a quizzical look. "What for?"

She pointed a thumb over her shoulder. "Roger heard what I said."

Emmett arched a brow. "It does take some getting used to."

"Tell me about it." She widened her eyes. "It took me years to feel comfortable with it myself. Oh, hey! I see firelight just ahead."

Emmett nodded. "Looks like we're here."

After asking around, they finally pulled up to Marian's home. Emmett jumped down from the wagon while Snow hurried to the back to check on the boy.

Emmett knocked on the door, and almost instantly his heart began racing. He was nervous about seeing his sister. So much was still unsettled between them. So much so that if he had known any other healer, he would not have come here. He turned around to look at Snow. Just the sight of her made him feel just a bit less tense.

The door swung open, and Emmett turned to find a giggling Marian with messy, curly hair and a disheveled dress. Robin Hood stood behind her with a naughty grin. Clearly, he had interrupted something. That would explain why it took his sister a few seconds to register who was standing at her door. Emmett wasn't particularly offended. After all, the night was dark, and he had grown a beard. So much had changed.

"Emmett?"

"Sorry to show up unannounced, but…" He motioned toward the wagon. "We need your help."

---

*M*arian came out of the bedroom with a slight crease between her brow, which often appeared when she was intensely focused. "He's going to be okay," she said, walking toward the basin in the kitchen and washing her hands. "The wound wasn't deep, but it was getting infected. I had to use the last of our medicine, but now he should start healing. It helps that wolves heal faster than most."

Emmett winced at the word "wolves."

He did it for the *child*.

"Thank you so much," Snow said, sitting at the table. He could tell a strange reluctance in her voice. Almost as if she wasn't comfortable being there. Good to know he wasn't the only one.

"If there's anything I can do to repay your kindness…"

"There might be," Marian said, taking a cloth from Robin's hand as he prepared dinner. "The entire kingdom is low on resources because of The Snow Queen's harsh winter. Now merchants are charging a lot more for herbs and medicine than we can afford."

More than she could afford? His sister was a princess, for crying out loud. If she had only stayed where she belonged, they wouldn't be going through financial problems. But Emmett decided to keep that to himself. "Why not just grow it yourself, now that winter has ended?" Emmett asked, taking a seat next to Snow at the table.

"Because…" Marian hesitated for a moment when Robin gave her a look. But then she turned away, apparently ignoring the silent warning Robin had given her. "*You* made it illegal for us to grow our own medicine. Punishable by death."

Emmett vaguely remembered agreeing to that law. It had been Prince John's idea.

"Can't Nathaniel undo that law?" he asked.

"He has to wait until he has a unanimous

concession from the counselors before changing the law, and it seems that many of them are still loyal to you, so they are making it hard for Nathaniel to undo the damage you've caused."

Emmett looked at his sister, unfazed. "He didn't seem to waste any time on changing the law on hunting wolves."

Marian gave her brother a stern look, but then Robin said something that broke their stare down. "Sorry, what?"

"The lobster," Robin repeated. "It's gone."

"What do you mean, it's gone?" Marian asked, looking around the room as if the animal had somehow crawled away.

Emmett caught Snow sinking in her chair, her eyes glued to her feet. As soon as she caught him looking, her cheeks reddened. He leaned close to her.

"Did you take the lobster?" he whispered.

"The poor thing was praying for the gods of the sea, Emmett," she whispered back. "What was I supposed to do?"

He leaned even closer, the flowery scent of her soap still lingering on her skin. "Where is he?"

Snow glanced across the room. Marian and Robin were too busy looking to pay attention to them. "I gave it to Roger so he could drop him back in the sea." She turned to meet Emmett's eyes. "I'm so sorry. I know it wasn't my place, and believe me, I feel terrible. I really do. But I couldn't just..." Her eyes lost their sparkle. "I couldn't ignore him."

Emmett nodded. He couldn't say he understood, but also couldn't imagine what it would feel like to hear an animal beg for his life. It was hard enough for an average person to hear a lobster scream as they're boiled alive, but to Snow, those screams would've sounded human.

He reached for her hand and gave it a light squeeze. "It's all right." He sat up in his chair and squared his shoulders. "Vegetables and potatoes sound like a pretty good dinner to me," he said, turning to look at his sister.

"Robin went through a lot of trouble to get that lobster," she said, giving him an accusing look.

Emmett shrugged. "I wasn't gonna eat it, anyway. I'm allergic to seafood," he said, pointing to the food that had already been placed at the table. "Now, shall we?"

Marian narrowed her eyes at him as though she didn't buy the lie, but then Robin put a hand on her shoulder and her expression softened. Emmett watched her follow Robin to the table where they seated themselves side by side. He and Snow joined them, and everyone settled into a polite silence. Robin served Marian, then Snow. Emmett insisted on making his own plate, but Robin made it for him, anyway. Reluctantly, Emmett accepted the food with a grateful nod. Then, for several minutes, the room fell quiet as everyone ate. Only the clinging of the spoon against the bowls filled the air.

"Since when are you allergic to seafood?" Marian asked, looking up from her bowl and giving him an accusatory stare. Emmett kept his expression neutral and focused on his food rather than meet her eyes.

"Since I got food poisoning a while back," he said, between bites. "Perhaps you would've known had you not ran away."

Marian's spoon banged against the table as

she slammed her fist on the hardwood. "Don't you dare."

Emmett lifted his eyes, innocently. "You asked."

"And *you* sold me off to that coward!" she yelled. "Like I was nothing but a signature in a contract! What did you expect me to do?"

A jolt of anger rippled through Emmett's body so fast, he pressed his eyes shut. He didn't want to lose control. He didn't come here for this. "I was being a king," he said through gritted teeth.

"You were being a selfish fool! Only thinking of yourself."

"Who else was I supposed to think of, Marian?" Emmett's blood boiled and he jumped to his feet, kicking back his chair. "There was no one left for me to care for! Those blazing wolves took everyone from me! They slaughtered our parents, injured my brother, then, to top it all off, they took *you*! I was left with *no one*!" Emmett's voice was so thunderous, the wooden walls just about shuddered. "Do you have any idea what it felt like to grieve alone? To wake up each day with a dagger of guilt stuck in your chest? Driving yourself mad, thinking you weren't strong enough to protect those you love?" His eyes blurred with tears, but he blinked them away. "So, yes. I know what kind of king I was, but after everything that happened, how could you expect me to be any different?"

Snow's eyes were like two fried eggs, and Robin reached for Marian's hand. The tenderness between Robin and Marian was almost too much.

Emmett stepped back, his hands shaking. "So, don't waste your breath telling me Nathaniel is twice the king I ever was, because I already know that," Emmett added, his voice deflating. "I was never groomed to be the leader of our kingdom. I had no guidance, but most importantly... I never asked for any of it."

He clenched his jaw, biting back the torrent of emotion rising in his chest. There was still so much he could say, but he was too spent.

Without another word, he turned around and headed out of the door.

*E*mmett had no idea how long he'd sat by the lake, but seeing that the moon had already started its descent, he figured it had been too long.

"There you are," Snow's soft voice came from behind him. He glanced over his shoulder to find her walking toward him.

"Sorry you had to see that." His voice was barely above a whisper.

"You have nothing to apologize for," she said, settling next to him and reaching for his hand. Her touch warmed him, and she clutched him with a softness that gripped his heart. The human contact was a luxury after spending so long alone, and her presence comforted him. Though he couldn't work out why. "Trust me. I've also had my share of family drama."

Emmett turned to meet her eyes. Despite them glistening with the reflection of the moon, they were filled with sadness. And Emmett thought what it must have been like to live in the cold palace with no one but The Snow Queen as family. However, though she was a vengeful, ice-spewing queen, she was the only family she had. "You miss your sister, don't you?"

She looked toward the lake with tears filling her eyes. "More than you'll ever know."

When she said nothing else, Emmett gave her hand a light squeeze. "You have a good heart, Snow."

She let out a chuckle, then wiped a tear that slid down her pale cheek. "I'm too weak to fight, Emmett. Thank you for offering, but I don't think I can follow through."

"Listen to me…" He turned to face her, then waited for her to look at him. When she did, he peered into her eyes. "The only thing stronger than physical strength… is the heart."

Snow smiled. "That's beautiful. Where did you hear that?"

He let out a soft chuckle. "Believe it or not, my brother. But that's not the point," he said quickly. "The point is… *you* have more heart than anyone I know. And for that alone, you can still win this fight."

Snow kept her eyes glued to his for a long moment, then she drew in a breath as if filling herself with renewed determination. "Then that's what I'll do," she said. "I'm going to fight with the heart instead of a sword."

Emmett smiled, admiring the strength he could already see in her. "How will you do that?"

"I'm not going to *destroy* my sister," Snow said. "I'm going to *save* her."

CHAPTER NINE

The next morning, Snow woke up to Roger's soft hoots. *Good morning, Princess.*

She stretched out like a cat and stifled a yawn as the weak morning sunshine floated into the room through cracks around the window. Marian insisted on giving her their spare bedroom upstairs—which was full of Robin's bows and weapons. Meanwhile, Emmett slept on the sofa in the living room.

Snow washed up and fixed her hair before she tiptoed down the creaky steps. When she peered around the corner, Emmett and Marian stood in the living room, heads bowed and talking to each other in low, dulcet tones.

"Take this," Emmett said, handing Marian a gold pocket watch.

Marian shook her head. "No, it was Father's. I can't…"

"Take it to the pawnshop and buy as much medicine as you can. I know Father wouldn't want me to hold onto this when there are people in need." Emmett placed his hand over Marian's and gave her a hard look, daring her to argue.

Her shoulders fell, and he pulled her in for a hug, then she buried her face in his neck with a sniff. "I'm sorry about the things I said yesterday," she said. "I never stopped to think about what you went through."

"That's all right. The past is the past."

"Not to me." She pulled back to look at him. "Not until we fix things between us. Between you and Nathaniel—"

"That's not going to happen, Marian."

"Why not?"

Emmett touched her arms, then looked into her eyes with a gentle gaze that clearly conveyed that he was done talking about it. "I'm glad I came. It was good to see you."

"Emmett—"

Snow walked in with a fake cough, hoping to save Emmett from a pressure that was plainly unwelcomed. "Morning!" she said, picking up her soft leather boots. Marian and Emmett broke apart.

"Are you both leaving... so soon?" Marian asked, watching Emmett as he marched over to pick up his jacket.

"Yeah, Snow and I have a long journey ahead."

"How's the boy doing?" Snow asked.

"He's fine," Marian replied. "Will and Red are coming over tonight. Perhaps they could find out who his parents are."

"That would be wonderful." Snow beamed. "Thank you."

The stairs creaked, and Robin's yawn broke their conversation.

"Just in time, sleepyhead," Marian said. "Our guests are leaving."

"Already?"

"We've stayed long enough," Emmett said, shrugging on his jacket.

"Going on another adventure, eh? Where are you off to this time?"

"The Ice Mountains," Snow said.

Robin dropped his hands and shook his head with a furious, "No, no, no. You're not."

"Robin nearly died at the Ice Mountains," Marian explained, her voice laced with concern. She wrung her hands and bit her lips as if trying to stop herself from saying more.

"And the mountain men," Robin cut in. "They're indestructible."

"We know the risks," Emmett added. "We'll be careful."

"At least let me prepare you a bag of food to take with you," Marian muttered, looking at Snow since Emmett was probably used to going without food for days.

"That would be lovely, thank you."

She marched off to the little kitchen while Robin wagged a finger at Emmett like he was a mischievous boy caught stealing apples at the market.

"What do you want to be going to the Ice Mountains for, anyway? You don't understand how dangerous it is—"

"We heard you the first time," Emmett cut in. He folded his arms and towered over Robin, his arms bulging in his jacket. "Besides, it's the only way for Snow to help her sister."

Robin snorted. "Aria? She's beyond help. Honestly, I wash my hands of that silly girl."

"Most people have, and I can't blame them," Snow said in a firm tone. "But I won't give up on her. You don't give up on family."

Robin crossed his arms and narrowed his eyes. "Even if you do manage to survive, you're not going to find anything to help you at the Ice Mountains."

Snow clamped her teeth together and began to grind them. Then she took a breath to steady her temper. She hated being looked at as the weak younger sister. "I'm going to bring Jack home."

Robin's face twisted at the sound of his name. "All that's waiting for you at the Ice Mountains are the mountain men and a terrible death."

"I'll take my chances," Snow said, determined. Robin hummed with disapproval, but Marian re-entered the room and handed Snow a cloth bag that was surprisingly heavy.

"It's not much, but it'll keep you going for a few days."

Snow broke eye contact with Robin and hugged Marian. "Thank you," she said into her wiry hair. When she pulled back to look at her, Marian's eyes were glassy.

"Be careful," she whispered.

"Don't worry, I'll protect her with my life," Emmett said.

Marian looked up at her brother and sniffed. "I want you *both* back alive," she said, giving her older brother a motherly look. "Because I need you to walk me down the aisle."

Emmett placed a hand over his heart, touched. "We'll be back. I give you my word."

Snow pulled on her cloak and swallowed as the air grew thick with emotion. But then Robin spoke a hundred miles an hour, giving Emmett advice about the Ice Mountains. "I'm telling you, those mountain men mean trouble. If you come across one, just run. Don't engage. Definitely don't shoot them. Arrows don't pierce their freaky skin."

Listening to Robin telling Emmett about the mountain men sent the hairs on the back of Snow's neck on end. She didn't know what they might face at the Ice Mountains, nor if they would survive the trip, but she knew one thing was certain. Jack was their only hope to bring Aria back to the good side.

Snow looked at Emmett, giving him a nod. "Time to go."

*R*obin had suggested they pack light and warned them that the paths were treacherous for a carriage to cross. So, Emmett pulled Snow onto Knight and sat behind her in the saddle. Feeling the warmth of his body against her back made Snow feel safe, despite the butterflies in her stomach.

When they stopped by a river, they dismounted. Knight neighed heavily. *I'm not as young as I once was. My back is killing me.* Then he greedily lapped up a drink from the river.

A twinge of guilt nipped at Snow's insides. "I want to walk from now on," she said to Emmett.

"What's wrong?" he said, searching her face.

Snow caressed the horse's mane. "Knight is tired."

"We've only been riding for a few hours,"

Emmett said, placing his hands on his hips, looking at his horse in disbelief.

I dragged that wagon for miles and miles, young man. Knight shook his head, puffing air through his nose. *I'm sore. And do I get any thanks for it? No.*

Snow bit against a growing smile. "Thank you."

"For what?" Emmett asked.

"Not you—I'm thanking Knight for dragging that heavy carriage to Sherwood." She rubbed the horse's mane and cooed at him.

Meanwhile, Emmett stared at Snow with his mouth hanging open, then dragged a hand through his hair with a sigh. "Well, I… I don't know what to say."

You could also thank me… for once. Snow nodded to Knight and hummed in agreement.

"What? What is he saying now?" Emmett demanded. Snow tickled Knight's ears as she looked at him. "He wants you to thank him too."

Emmett dropped his hand with a breathy laugh and looked around, a rush of color rising to his temples. "I'm not talking to a horse," he said, his voice weak.

"Why not?" Snow asked, tilting her head as she studied Emmett.

He paced around and opened his mouth, but nothing came out except a hiss. "It's... I... well..." He exhaled as he pinched the bridge of his nose. "Thank you, Knight."

Snow grinned. "See, that wasn't so hard, was it?"

After several hours—with intermittent breaks—Snow and Emmett finally emerged from the forest and came out to a ravine. A glistening ice bridge stretched across it, leading to the vast white mountains looming over them like sleeping giants.

Emmett whistled as they took in the scenery. "So, these are the Ice Mountains. They look a lot bigger from here than they did from my kingdom."

Snow nodded, unable to talk. He was right. Just the snowy tips of the mountains could be seen from the Chanted Forest. She imagined that Emmett would have had the same view from his castle.

The people shared folk tales about the Ice Mountains, but no one dared to climb them, for every curious traveler that went was never seen again.

"You know, the dwarfs used to tell stories about the mountain men," Snow said as they crossed the bridge. A gust of wind howled up from the bottom of the ravine, and the air grew so cold that it had a frosty bite to it. Snow wrapped her cloak tighter around her shoulders and tried not to let her teeth chatter.

"So, what did the dwarfs have to say about them?" Emmett asked, strolling along like they were having a pleasant walk in the woods. Even though the only thing preventing them from plunging to their deaths was an ice bridge that, judging by the too-perfect design, was fashioned by her sister.

"They said the mountain men were ancient humans that lived in camps. One day, a tribe was caught in an avalanche, but not an ordinary avalanche. It was formed by a powerful king who wanted to build an unstoppable army."

Emmett hummed deeply. "Robin did say arrows don't hurt them."

Snow nodded as they reached the other side and she lowered her voice to a whisper.

"They do not feel fear nor pain, and they have the strength to tear a... a... wolf limb from limb."

Emmett shot her an amused look. "*Limb from limb*? That's a bit violent, don't you think?"

Snow's cheeks pinched. "I'm only repeating what they said."

The skies grew white and tiny flecks of snow fell to the ground. "Well, I don't suppose they told you how to defeat them, did they?" Emmett asked.

Snow shook her head and lifted the hood of her cloak, desperate for warmth as they followed a narrow path between two mountains.

I don't like this. I don't like this at all, Knight muttered as they walked deeper through the pass. Snow shushed him and stroked his mane, trying to offer him comfort. Emmett stopped by a narrow path leading up one of the mountains and crouched down.

"Have you found anything?" Snow asked him, her voice barely audible over the high winds.

Emmett craned his head to give her a

frown. "You won't believe what tracks I've found."

Snow edged closer to peer at the prints on the snowy floor. "They look like…"

"Bear prints," Emmett finished. "But a bear bigger than anything I've ever seen."

Snow gulped. "You know I love animals," she whispered in his ear. "But I don't know if I want to meet the bear that made these tracks."

Emmett rose to his feet, bracing against the winds and took Knight's reins. "Well, that's too bad, because these tracks are fresh and they are leading the way."

Snow stared open-mouthed as Emmett led Knight up the rocky path. "Why do we need to follow that?" Snow asked, picking up the rear.

"Because," Emmett shouted over his shoulder as they pressed on, "they're going to lead us safely up the mountain."

"How do you figure that?" Snow's black hair whipped across her face, and she clung onto the narrow tree trunks as they continued to climb forward. When she puffed her hair out of her eyes, she caught Emmett smirking at her.

"If a giant bear made it up okay, I'm sure Knight will be able to as well," he said.

Oh, great. I feel so much better about this climb now, Knight grumbled. Snow chuckled at his sarcasm. *I suppose the fact that a bear has more agile limbs than me doesn't make a difference?*

Luckily, the path wound inward as the mountain opened up and the steep walls on either side shielded them from the harsh winds. Up ahead there was a fork in the road, and each path rose up opposite sides of the mountain. Snow and Emmett searched the ground for clues to show them which fork to take.

"The bear prints lead up that way," Emmett said, pointing to the fork on the right. Snow knelt down and looked at a different set of prints. A squirrel scurried along the ground.

Must get back home. So very cold.

"Excuse me," Snow whispered, and the squirrel's ears pricked up. It stopped and looked up at her, its little body shivering. Snow held out her hand. "Hop on and I'll warm you up for a few moments."

The squirrel hesitated and sniffed her

hand with curiosity. He then scurried up her arm and buried himself in her cloak, wrapping his little body up with his fluffy tail. "I wonder... have you seen any men on this mountain?" Snow asked, keeping her voice soft. She knew that squirrels had very sensitive ears and even a whisper sounded like a roar in the wind. Roger would have been an invaluable aid to them, but she didn't want anything to happen to him, so she instructed him to stay behind.

Emmett was standing next to Knight, removing a sheepskin bottle from his saddle. He took a steady gulp of water, unaware of Snow's little friend.

Men, you say? the squirrel replied. *Why, I see lots of them in these parts, but none of them are as warm and friendly as you are.*

"Do you know of any camps?"

Camps?

Snow nodded. "Tents. Burning fires. Humans?"

The squirrel wriggled against her neck. *I see smoke rising over that side of the mountain most nights. Maybe there is a camp there.*

Snow looked up. The direction the squirrel

was referring to would lead them to take the fork on the left. "Thank you. Would you like to join me for a little while? Is your home very far?"

No, no. Thank you for the warmth. I must go back to my family.

The squirrel ran down Snow's body, and if it weren't for the fact she was numb from the cold, she would have giggled. "I say we go left," she said, turning back to Emmett now that the squirrel was gone.

"But the bear went right," he said, handing her a drink. "Why do you want to go left?"

Snow would have told Emmett about the squirrel, but he had already looked at her like she was crazy once before. Besides, she was unsure how convinced he would be to take advice from an animal.

"That path over there looks more traveled."

Emmett swiveled his head to look. "It looks pretty untouched to me."

Snow marched forward and surreptitiously pressed her heel in the snow. "Look, human footprints!"

Emmett joined her with Knight by his side. His gaze pointed at the ground, then he gave Snow a frank look. "It's *one* footprint... and it's yours."

Snow's cheeks heated.

"Can you tell me why you're insisting on going this way?"

Snow stepped back, feeling small under Emmett's discerning stare. But when she didn't reply, he dropped his hands and smiled softly at her. "Look. I'm here to keep you safe. If you want to go this way, then that's the way we'll go."

Snow perked up and lifted her head. "Right. Then come on." She marched forward, a smile creeping across her lips.

Soon, the clouds grew dark, and the harsh winds slapped Snow's cheeks until they were red raw. Knight drew weary and complained with every step. Snow knew that soon they would have to find a place to rest for the night.

Emmett must have had the same thought because just as they reached the crest of a small hill, he held up his fist and halted. "Knight is tired, and the weather is terrible," he said. "We should find a place to rest."

Oh, what I'd give to be back home in a nice warm stable. I'll never complain about the crickets keeping me up at night again, Knight mumbled with an irritated neigh. Emmett shushed him, and even though he could not hear Knight's thoughts, he seemed to sense his feelings.

"All right, there's got to be shelter somewhere," Snow said, looking around the trees. A mature fern tree offered a dry patch of grass, and Knight bolted to it. Emmett and Snow were about to follow, but a piercing cry stopped them in their tracks.

"What was that?" Snow hurried to stand close to Emmett. He pulled out his axe and handed her his knife.

"Sounds like we've got company," he muttered.

Snow gripped the knife with both hands, wishing she had trained more before she attempted this adventure.

"We mean you no harm," Emmett called out. "We're just looking for safe passage."

"What a mighty relief. We were all so scared," an eerie voice carried in the wind.

Snow shivered, but this time it had nothing to do with the chill in the air. She whipped around, disoriented, but found no one. Emmett and Snow stood back-to-back, looking around, searching for the owners of the eerie voice that surrounded them.

"I thought you meant no harm? Yet, you brought weapons," another voice said, sounding far too close for comfort.

The winds died down just enough for her to see a man step into view. Her eyes met the steely eyes of the bald man who must have been almost seven feet tall. His entire body was painted white with strange markings along his legs. Snow's hands trembled as she clung to the knife like it was a lifeline.

"We don't want any trouble," Emmett said, keeping his voice low. Snow nodded quickly as more men encircled them. Before long, they were completely surrounded, and Snow wondered what a knife would do against their impenetrable skin.

Please. Somebody help us! Snow screamed silently. Her whole body flooded with foolishness. What was she thinking, venturing to the Ice Mountains when she knew full well that rarely anyone returned. For all she knew, Jack wasn't even there anymore and it was a wasted journey.

"You're warm," one of the mountain men said, stepping close to her and dragging a bony finger down the side of her face. It left a burning trail as if he had scalded her. Snow's breath hitched, and Emmett's back flinched against hers.

"Don't touch her!" he shouted. "Or I'll—"

"You will taste good when I've cooked you," the same mountain man replied. His words sank like rocks to the bottom of Snow's stomach. When Robin warned her about the mountain men, she never dreamed it was because they were cannibals.

"Hold still, and I'll make sure to cut this pretty throat nice and clean so you bleed out real fast."

Before the man could raise a knife, Snow thrust Emmett's silver blade into the mountain man's chest. To her surprise, the knife sank into his skin with a terrible crunch. Snow pulled it out and gasped as the mountain man stumbled backward, holding his chest and looking at the gleaming red drops of blood on his fingers with confusion. It seemed that the mountain men's impenetrable skin was no match for elven steel, but they were still vastly outnumbered. Emmett seemed to follow Snow's train of thought and gripped the handle of his axe with a grunt.

"Get down!" he roared to Snow, then he swung the axe in a circle around them, hitting all the mountain men with a succession of thuds and clangs. A pile of groaning bodies hit the ground.

Emmett grasped Snow's hand. "Run!"

They sprinted past the fallen men, and Snow hardly dared to look back. As they reached Knight, Emmett threw Snow onto the horse's back and hopped on the saddle in front of her. "I know you're tired, buddy, but we need you," Snow said to him.

Knight screeched, panting air through his nostrils, then galloped up the path.

Snow clung onto Emmett's chest, pressing her body up to his back like her life depended on it. She glanced back to find the men rising to their feet and running toward them like a stampede of elephants. The ground trembled beneath them, and the ear-splitting screams filled Snow's body with adrenaline.

"Keep going, Knight! Don't stop!" Emmett said as they charged through the trees.

Snow glanced back to find that the mountain men were catching up. The ground steepened and Knight struggled to keep his footing on the loose gravel. Knight staggered and Snow yelped, almost falling off. Emmett grabbed her by the arm and secured her hands around his waist. Once they reached the top of the hill, Snow squinted through the blizzard at the mountain men who now crawled on all fours like giant glacier spiders, gaining speed.

When they clawed Knight's hind, he ripped out a painful screech and rose onto his back legs. Snow slipped, but Emmett held her tightly as she dangled off the horse's saddle. She looked ahead and spotted a dozen more mountain men blocking their path.

Knight dropped to all fours again, and Snow shut her eyes, clutching to Emmett with a death grip. "I'm so sorry," she sobbed as the mountain men inched forward.

"No. We're not going like this," Emmett roared. He then took his silver blade and hopped down from Knight. Snow watched with her heart in her mouth as Emmett slashed at the men one by one, slitting their cold skin, knocking the mountain men off their feet and throwing them off the edge of the mountain.

Snow could hardly breathe as she watched him work. Emmett was fierce and marched into danger without an ounce of fear. He gave a battle cry as he slammed his knife into his foes, and for a moment, Snow thought they might have a chance of surviving.

But then she spotted one mountain man that was scrambling over the edge and grasped Emmett's boot. Snow jumped down, fueled by adrenaline, grabbed the knife from Emmett and thrust it into the mountain man's hand. The elven blade pierced into his thick skin, and an ear-piercing scream ripped through his throat. He let go of Emmett, then slid off the edge.

Snow helped Emmett to his feet, then they stood back-to-back once more. She knew there was no hope. Soon, they would be overtaken and forced to face the most terrible death imaginable.

A new sound sent a shockwave over the whole mountain top, and for a split second, the mountain men stopped and looked around, wondering what was happening.

An almighty roar flooded the air and the ground trembled as a ferocious white beast charged into view. Snow's mouth hung open and Emmett lowered his axe as they came face to face with the largest polar bear Snow had ever seen.

It burst through the mountain men, sending them flying over the edge like pebbles. When it opened its gigantic jaws, they were sprayed with saliva so frigid, it froze them on the spot. The few mountain men that could move scattered, and soon Emmett and Snow were the only ones left standing on the mountain top.

They stood panting, both too shocked to move or speak, as the polar bear puffed air through his nose and bowed his head.

"You saved us," Snow said, reaching out to touch the bear. But then the creature looked at her, its eyes glowing blue, and Snow covered her mouth in shock.

The bear was not an animal at all. And

just as the realization struck, the bear crumpled into a huge pile of snow.

"What on Earth was that?" Emmett asked, placing his axe back and inspecting what was left of the bear.

Snow looked up at the gloomy sky, and bit against the tears welling in her eyes.

"That…" She didn't know how it was possible, but there was only one explanation. "Was Aria."

CHAPTER TEN

The blizzard was getting stronger, and Emmett was exhausted from the battle. He was certain that Snow's energy was spent too. They took cover in a nearby cave that Knight had found and Emmett started a fire. Good thing Marian had packed food for them to take. He was famished and there was nothing growing on that barren mountain. Snow had barely nibbled the corner of her flatbread. She hadn't been the same since the ice monster showed up to get rid of the mountain men.

"You have to eat more," Emmett said between bites. "You'll need to build up your strength if we're going to keep going up the mountain."

Snow nodded, but continued to stare at the food, not eating. "How did she do it?" she asked, lifting her eyes to look at Emmett across the fire. "How did she know we were in trouble?"

"Maybe she didn't," Emmett said with a shrug. "I heard rumors that those creatures were created on her coronation day. I assume after the winter passed, they all came here in order not to melt."

Her shoulders sagged, and she looked into the fire with sadness in her eyes.

"Sorry, did I say something wrong?" Emmett asked.

"Not at all." Snow flashed him a sad smile. "It's just that the coronation day brings back very bad memories for me."

Emmett leaned back on the rocky wall and crossed his legs at the ankles. "Want to talk about it?"

She hesitated for a moment, but then met his eyes once more. "That was when *The Snow Queen* began to rule," she said. "And she took the man I love away from me."

Emmett dropped his bread. Something about hearing her loving another man made him lose his appetite. Though he wasn't sure why. He wasn't there to win her heart. He was hired to keep her safe. That was it. "Did she kill him?"

"At first, I thought she did. But she actually pushed him into a portal to another world," Snow explained. "It's called Oxford. The same place Jack came from."

"That doesn't sound like a bad place."

"That's not the point," Snow snapped, and Emmett wondered if she could somehow detect the indifference in his tone. It wasn't fair to her that he wished the lover boy stayed gone. With all the trauma she had been through, Emmett wanted her to have everything her heart desired. He couldn't think of anyone more deserving of happiness.

"You're right," he said, giving her a gentle look. "I'm sorry."

"No, I'm sorry..." She shook off the scowl. "It's just that those memories are very painful. I didn't just lose George that day. I lost my sister too."

"Did she ever tell you why she did it?" he asked.

Snow shook her head. "All she's ever said was that it was for my own good."

Emmett arched a skeptical brow. "That's it?"

"That's it."

A gust of wind blew through the cave so unexpectedly, Snow yelped and wrapped her arms around herself. The fire that had been burning vanished, and in the blink of an eye, they were both sitting in the dark. Emmett thought about reaching for her, but he wasn't sure if that was a good idea. He didn't want her to think he was making a move. But then her hands patted his leg.

"I'm right here," he said, reaching for her hand and guiding her to where he was sitting.

"I can't see anything," she said, settling next to him. "And how did the temperature drop so fast?"

He was about to respond when her body pressed up against his side and her arms wrapped around his stomach.

"The blizzard is getting stronger," he said, stating the obvious because clearly his brain was too stunned at their sudden proximity. Her body shivered, and he threw his cloak over her shoulders. He then wrapped his arms around her petite frame and pulled her close. "It should warm up by morning."

"I would just be happy to make it through the night," she said through her chattering teeth.

"We will," he said, rubbing the palm of his hand over her arm. "We just have to keep warm."

In the dark, the horse's hooves echoed in the cave, and suddenly the icy chill diverted from them. Though there was still a chill in the air, the frigid winds no longer hit them head-on. Emmett didn't have to see to know that Knight had laid down in the direct path of the wind, blocking the frigid blow.

"Good boy, Knight," Emmett whispered.

The horse snorted.

"He says you're welcome," Snow replied, no longer shivering. Still, she pressed her face into his chest. He tightened his arms around her and rested his stubbled cheek atop her head.

Being that close to her had never crossed

his mind. Mainly because he was with her under false pretenses. He'd been hired to keep her from coming to any harm. That was his job. *She* was his job. She was also still a princess, while he was no longer a king. So, no matter what happened, he would never return to the palace. He would live the rest of his days as far away from his brother's kingdom as possible and pursue the life of a huntsman. That was his future, and she deserved so much more than the life of an outcast.

After a few seconds, he found himself wondering out loud, "Is that really what he said?"

Snow giggled, and the horse neighed.

Emmett suppressed a smile. "That's what I thought."

---

*B*y morning, the blizzard had passed, and the sky was a clear blue. As soon as the sun began to rise, Emmett helped Snow onto the horse, but he himself walked ahead, pulling Knight along.

"Where are we headed now?" Snow asked.

"I was thinking we should pick a direction and see where it takes us." Saying it aloud sounded a lot more foolish than it did in his head, but Snow was nice enough not to call him out on it. He glanced up at her, and she simply flashed him a smile.

"I may have a better idea," she said with a wink. Then she sat up straight and whistled to the sky. It was a lovely sound, like a bird's song. When she finished, there was a long moment of silence. Then the chirping of birds filled the air, the melodic sound traveling all over the mountain.

Snow kept nodding as if taking in careful instructions. Emmett watched her, trying to read her expression. But all he was able to focus on was the dimple indenting her cheek. Suddenly, thoughts of having her in his arms again flooded his mind. He'd never thought he would have gotten so close to her, but now that he had, the thought played on a loop.

"They said there's a tribe in a valley one day's journey from here," Snow said, snapping Emmett from his thoughts. He looked in the direction she pointed. The valley didn't seem unreasonably far. He let out a long breath, then pulled Knight along.

---

*T*he terrain changed as they walked farther down the mountain path. Where there was once icy barren ground now stood small overgrown bushes lining the trail. Dirt and stones crunched underneath Emmett's boots, and after a steep climb, they came out onto a small valley of fern trees and lush green grass dancing in the wind.

By the time they arrived at the valley, the sky had grown dark and painted-faced people danced around a bonfire. Judging by the beating drums and their chants, Emmett supposed they had walked in on an important ceremony.

As soon as they came into view, everyone stopped and stared at them. They made Emmett's mud streaks look like child's play. Those were some serious, intricate symbols they displayed on their skin.

A young man with a long braid of black

hair stepped in front of Emmett. "How can we help you?"

Emmett placed a gentle hand on Knight's nose, and he stopped. "We're looking for someone," he replied to the man. "His name is Jack."

The man's eyes widened in surprise. "Frost?"

Emmett glanced at Snow for confirmation. He'd never heard that name before, but then again, he wasn't familiar with Jack.

"Yes," Snow replied. "With snowy white hair."

The man gave them a terse smile. "Come with me." When he turned and began to walk, the tribe continued their dance around the fire. Emmett's muscles tensed, but he pushed himself to follow, keeping a hand on the hilt of his knife. They had already crossed danger once on their trip, and he knew nothing of this tribe and their intentions.

Once they arrived, the young man disappeared into a tent made of animal hide. Emmett walked to the side of the horse and looked up at Snow.

"Are you sure about this?" he asked, keeping his voice low.

"Not really," she muttered back. "But what other choice do we have?"

She had a point, but he still wasn't comfortable trusting the strange man. He stretched out his arms, and she jumped down. He caught her in midair, and when her chest pressed against him, he found himself not wanting to let her go. He held her gaze for a long moment, trying to discern if perhaps she felt the same way.

Suddenly, struck by the reality of their situation, he winced. This sudden shift in his feelings was becoming a problem, and it would only get worse once all of it was over and she had to return to the palace. He was leaving for the Northern Realm. And no amount of feelings could change that.

He placed her on the ground, then hurried to grab Knight's reins to tie him to a wooden post a few feet away. The whole time he was making the knot, he sensed her gaze on him. But when he turned around, she averted her eyes.

He walked toward the entrance of the tent, then turned to Snow. "Shall we?"

She walked past him, and he followed her inside.

The tent was bigger than it appeared from the outside. A scatter of cushions encircled a small wooden table in the center. The young man stood aside as an older man sat in front of the table, surrounded by candles and burning incense, with his legs crossed and eyes closed in a meditating position.

The old man had deep lines around his mouth and between his brows. His wiry gray hair was scraped back into a tight bun atop his head, and he had an array of colors painted in intricate designs on his face and arms.

Snow went to stand next to the young man, who squared his shoulders and held his hands behind his back. Emmett followed her lead.

"Who's this?" Emmett whispered to the young man.

"Our chieftain," he whispered back. "He has spent a great amount of time with Frost."

"Leave us," the chieftain spoke, not bothering to open his eyes.

"But Chief?"

"I said... leave us."

"Yes, sir." The young man bowed his head respectfully, then backed out of the tent.

"Please," the chieftain said, motioning to the space in front of him. "Take a seat."

Emmett and Snow shared a quick glance, then Snow went to sit across from the old man. Emmett followed and settled next to her.

The old man rested his open palms upward on his knee. "You seek answers."

"Yes," Snow replied. "We're seeking to find Jack Frost. We need his help."

"A very special gift was bestowed on Frost," the old man said, finally opening his eyes and looking at Snow. "And I sense the same for you."

Snow's mouth parted. "Me?"

Emmett didn't like the way the man was looking at Snow. As if he could see through her. The man smiled.

"Keep on seeking, and you shall find."

Snow gave the man a quizzical look. "What will I find?"

"Freedom," he said, giving her a knowing

look. "To achieve the victory you seek, you must first seek answers with an open mind."

"What kind of answers?" Emmett cut in, narrowing his eyes at the chieftain. He didn't like the cryptic lines one bit.

Snow touched Emmett's hand as if encouraging him to trust the old man. "Freedom from what?" she asked.

"Your sister." The chieftain pointed to something on the tablet between him and Snow. It was a hand mirror that lay face down. Emmett hadn't noticed it was there before. "And the truth..." the chieftain added, "shall set you free."

Snow hesitated, but only for a moment. When she reached for the hand mirror, a wave of discomfort rose inside Emmett. The etchings carved in the silver frame matched the handle of his silver blade, which meant it had to be made of elven metal.

"It's another Mirror of Reason," Snow muttered under her breath. Emmett leaned over to take a better look. From what Snow had told him about her sister's mirror, that one didn't look like it could have been a portal. No human would ever be able to fit through it. Maybe it served another purpose?

Snow lifted her eyes to look at the chieftain, waiting for further instructions. Emmett scooted closer to her. If anything happened, he needed to be close enough to grab her and run.

The chieftain leaned forward and waved a hand over the mirror in Snow's hands. "Show her that which will set her free."

The silver frame began to glow, and Snow stared at it with eyes unblinking. Then her reflection in the mirror faded and the image of a baby took its place.

It was a baby girl so young, not even her hair had grown yet. Her eyes were closed in a peaceful sleep as she was cradled by a man with long, silver hair. By the crease between Snow's brows, it didn't seem like she recognized the man. He wore a crown made of shells, and he held the baby against his bare chest. His skin was wet, and his lower body was hidden beneath the water. But then an iridescent fin came into view and Snow gasped.

"Merman," she muttered. Emmett leaned

closer to get a better angle at the images in motion.

Snow kept her unblinking eyes on the mirror. With glistening tears falling from his clear blue eyes, the merman handed the baby girl to an old man that Emmett had never seen before. He took the sleeping baby in his arms and walked away, leaving the merman to cry silently while floating in the water.

When the image vanished and Snow's reflection returned, Emmett noticed a single tear slid down her porcelain cheek. The chieftain made a sound of approval, as though her distress was precisely what he wanted. He returned to his meditative state.

Without another word, Snow placed the mirror on the ground, jumped to her feet, and ran out of the tent, crying.

Emmett ran after her. "Snow, wait!"

She darted into the forest, and Emmett followed the sound of rustling leaves and her footsteps. When he came to a small lake, he found her standing at the edge, her shoulders trembling. The full moon above reflected on the water casting an ethereal glow. Though she kept her back to Emmett, he could hear her cries.

"What happened back there?" he asked.

She turned around, wiping her eyes. "I'll tell you what happened," she replied, sniffling. "I was just shown the *truth*."

Emmett had no idea what she was talking about. "What truth?"

"The truth that sets me free from my sister," she repeated the chieftain's words. "That was it. Didn't you see it?"

No, he hadn't. He stared at her, his heart aching as she broke apart before his eyes.

"That baby was me, Emmett," she said. "And that was my biological father. He gave me away to The Intruder."

"Your biological father was a merman?" Emmett echoed in disbelief. "That doesn't make any sense. How does that set you free?"

Snow shook her head. "I'm not royal, Emmett." Her voice was barely above a whisper. "Which means I'm free from the fight with The Snow Queen. I have no right to the throne unless I kill her. And I can't. *I won't*—kill anyone."

Emmett hated that she was hurting, but

something about her not being a princess filled him with a selfish hope. They weren't so different after all.

"All my life…" she muttered, turning away. "I've always followed the rules. I've always done what was asked of me. I've always been proper as a princess should be. And for what?"

Emmett frowned, wishing there was something he could say to soothe her broken heart. To take all the pain away.

"You know what…" She wiped her wet face, then squared her shoulders. "If all this was meant to set me free, then… that's exactly what it'll do." She turned to Emmett with renewed determination. "I'm done being proper. I'm done following the rules."

Before Emmett even took another breath, she grabbed his face and pressed her lips to his.

CHAPTER ELEVEN

*A*ll sense of reason fizzled away as Snow pressed her lips to Emmett's. But when he stiffened under her, Snow pulled back and lifted her hand to her mouth.

"I am so sorry," she whispered, horror creeping in at Emmett's shocked expression.

Emmett had treated her well and had been so sweet, but perhaps he hadn't made a move on her because he simply didn't find her attractive. She turned away, unable to look him in the eyes.

"I'm so, *so* sorry." She buried her face in her hands. "I am mortified."

Emmett touched her shoulder, and when he spoke, his voice was soft in her ear. "You are the one person in this world who has no reason to be sorry. Now, please, look at me."

Snow shook her head, her face still buried in her hands. "I can't. It's too embarrassing."

"I actually thought it was pretty arousing." She didn't have to look at him to know he was grinning.

Her cheeks burned even hotter. "Emmett, you're not helping."

"Snow, can you please show me your face so I can kiss you back?"

Snow dropped her hands and turned to meet his eyes. "You *want* to kiss me back?" she asked, surprised.

He smiled. "Of course I want to kiss you." He drew close and cupped her face. "I've been wanting to kiss you."

"Then why haven't you?"

"I was afraid." He held her gaze for a long moment, all the while brushing his thumb over her cheek like she was a delicate flower. That simple touch made her feel so safe with him.

"Afraid of what?" she asked.

He shook his head. "None of that matters anymore," he said in an almost growl. Snow's stomach tangled as he enveloped her body with his muscular arms. A waft of his woody scent rushed through her whole body, rendering her knees useless, and she buckled, but he was there to catch her.

He hovered his mouth less than an inch from hers as he held her tight. A soft groan escaped his throat, and it drove her senses wild.

Snow searched his eyes for any sign that he wanted to stop, but instead, she saw hunger. The desire written all over every beautiful curvature of his face. She dragged her hands through his thick hair and tugged on it, pulling him closer.

With their bodies pressed against each other, it was impossible to notice the frosty air and swirling winds around them. Instead, heat sizzled from their bodies as they puffed clouds into the air.

Snow didn't know who she was anymore. Playing the role as Aria's little sister was over. She wasn't even a princess. But even with the ache of uncertainty, she knew exactly what she wanted to happen next.

With a careful balance between fierce protection and tenderness, Emmett's gaze lingered on her mouth. She licked her lips instinctively, and when she pressed her body against his chest, an entirely new desire awakened. Like fireworks lighting up every part of her mind.

"Snow, there is something you must——" Emmett began, but Snow shushed him with her lips.

"I thought you said you wanted to kiss me?" she whispered against his mouth.

"I do."

"Then stop talking." She caught a flash of excitement in Emmett's eyes as he grinned against her mouth. Then, in one swift move, he lifted her up in the air, squeezing her waist. She lowered her face to meet his lips again, and as her tongue found his, the hunger grew tenfold.

Emmett moaned and it was the most primal, delightful sound. Snow nipped his bottom lip, then sucked on it until he made that gorgeous sound again.

Suddenly, all her fears and worries became small and insignificant as they explored each other's mouths, exchanging kisses and tasting the delicious taste of passion. Until minutes passed and Snow grew light-headed. She needed to come up for air, but the way Emmett took over the kiss sent her wild. So what if she passed out?

But just as black spots covered her vision and her lungs screamed for air, her feet found the ground and Emmett released her mouth.

Snow trembled from head to toe as she took deep breaths, the rush of ice-cold air cooling her heated body. Emmett's eyes locked on her, and a slightly wicked smile crossed his face.

Under the blanket of the night's sky, Snow stole courage and grinned back. Like two opposing magnets, they joined at the hip once more, and Snow's hands found the back of Emmett's neck. She twirled his hair between her fingers and bit her lip as Emmett closed his arms around her again.

"What do you want to do…?" Emmett murmured, his breath heating her lips. Snow was giddy at the question. She had never been this intimate with anyone. Not even with George. They had kissed, but never that intensely. She pushed every thought of George away, then waited for a wave of guilt to wash over her, but it never came.

Things had changed. She was in the Ice Mountains, a forbidden part of the world, with a man who she wanted to do forbidden things with. But then humor sparkled in Emmett's eyes.

"Snow…" He suppressed a smile. "I meant about Jack."

A mixture of disappointment and foolishness washed over Snow, and although she tried releasing him from her grip, he kept her secured in his arms. She had left the tent before she had a moment to even ask about Jack's whereabouts.

"I don't know," she breathed.

Emmett rubbed small circles on her lower back, sensing her tension. "We could keep looking for him. Or…"

"Or what?" Snow asked, blinking up into his eyes. His brows pinched and a little line formed between his eyes as he hummed, conflicted.

She wondered if he had another plan in mind. One that didn't involve Jack, or Aria.

One that sent them traveling to a faraway land and setting up a new life together.

Just the thought made Snow's heart flutter. But then a sinking sensation took hold of her stomach at the memory of Aria creating the ice monsters all over the kingdom. And her alliance with Prince John. Marian lacking medicine. The dwarfs lacking food. People she cared about were suffering. And she was sure it was just the beginning. If Aria didn't come back to her senses soon, surely she would travel so far down the evil path that there would be no hope left for the kingdom.

Even if she wasn't her blood sister, Snow wanted Aria to find her happiness, which would then allow the kingdom to live in peace. Something that the people of the Chanted Forest hadn't experienced for decades.

"We need to find Jack," Snow said, giving in. "But after that… anything is possible." She smiled and Emmett's eyes brightened.

"Come on, let's get some sleep," he said, pressing his lips to the back of her hand. Flutters filled her stomach as they walked back to the village holding hands.

Knight had been moved to a tent closer to

the forest. He snorted softly and it echoed in the quiet night. It was so still that Snow couldn't even hear an owl hooting.

The villagers set up this tent for you two since you're friends of Jack Frost, Knight said. *They also left food inside.*

Snow gulped nervously, then noticed Emmett looking at her. "Looks like this tent is for us," she said, hoping he wouldn't notice the shakiness in her voice. Moments ago, she would've let him do whatever he wanted to her, but now that she had recovered, and her senses had returned, the boldness was gone.

Emmett offered her a soft smile as he cupped her face. "I don't know about you, but I'm exhausted and looking forward to a good night's sleep."

He was being a gentleman, and the nervousness vanished. She smiled. "I'm pretty spent, myself."

"Then sleep it is," he said innocently. He took her hand and pulled her into the tent. It was a lot more spacious than they needed it to be. A small pile of food and drinks sat in the corner while two rolled-out blankets sat in the center.

Emmett lay on one of the blankets, then patted the other. Snow gave a bashful smile, but before she could lay next to him, Knight entered the tent and pushed past her, settling on the other side of her blanket.

Snow giggled as she lay in between her two knights.

"Let me guess…" Emmett said, narrowing his eyes at his horse. "Her owl told you to keep an eye on her?"

"See?" Snow caressed Knight's mane while looking at Emmett. "They aren't all that hard to understand."

Emmett gave his horse a playful look of betrayal. "You're my horse. Aren't you supposed to be looking out for *me*?"

Knight snorted, and Snow turned to Emmett with a smug look. "He says he likes me better."

"All this time I thought, 'Hey, at least I've got my horse. He doesn't judge me.' And now I find out he does." Emmett watched her for a long moment. "Though, I can't blame him for liking you more."

Snow snuggled her back against Emmett's chest and used his bicep as her pillow.

"Goodnight, Princess," he whispered in her ear, draping a heavy arm around her. Snow shuddered with delight, encased in his warmth, and let her heavy lids flutter to a close.

"I'm not a princess, remember?" she whispered back.

Emmett stroked her hair, sending little shocks of pleasure through her spent body. "You'll always be a princess to me."

---

*E*mmett and Snow thanked the villagers for their hospitality and followed the map drawn out for them to find Jack's village. The weather was more pleasant, and a few birds chirped as they flew over their heads.

Snow stumbled on some loose gravel, and Emmett found her hand as quick as a Venus flytrap. Snow blushed, and when Emmett didn't let go as they continued to walk, she was startled at how natural it was to hold his hand.

They finally reached another hilltop, and the sound of wind instruments floated up to them. There was snow on the ground once more and a different kind of chill in the air. As they drew closer to a settlement, Snow's gaze landed on a group of men sitting around a fire while the women sat in a huddle, washing clothes in a spring of steaming water.

Snow scanned the pale faces of the people, dressed in fine silks. This tribe looked starkly different from the one they had encountered the night before. Each person had silver-white hair just like Jack.

As they approached, a young man turned, and his glacier eyes bore into her. It took her brain a few beats to process who was standing there. He was strong, and healthy, and stood with an authority and a presence that made her feel small. But there was no mistaking him.

"Jack!" She broke from Emmett's hand and ran into Jack's outstretched arms. He held her tenderly as a bubble of emotion rose to the base of her throat, making it hard to swallow.

Flashes of dark memories took hold of her mind, and Jack cradled her like a big brother soothing his little sister.

"What brings you all this way?" he asked when they broke apart. His gaze landed on Emmett, who had caught up. "I see you've found your prince charming."

Snow gave Jack a quizzical look. "What?"

Jack's face broke into an amused smile, then he shook his head. "Never mind."

Emmett held out his hand. "I'm Emmett, not a prince but a hunter." They shook hands and Jack's face turned to mild surprise.

"So... Snow White and the huntsman. Now, that's an interesting twist."

Snow and Emmett exchanged looks, then she gave him a bashful smile. She had not warned him that sometimes Jack spoke in cryptic ways.

"Did you find what you were looking for?" Snow asked him. She knew he'd come searching for his ancestors. Peering over his shoulder at the people at the camp, Snow figured he did. But Jack looked down, his expression growing dark.

"Yes. I've discovered who I was meant to become. I always thought Jack Frost was just a legend, though I suppose after discovering that fairy tales are real, I shouldn't have been surprised. Nevertheless, I could never imagine I could belong to this world." He rubbed his chin, looking at the ground, and snowflakes fell in the space between them. "There is still so much to learn. It could take a lifetime."

Snow wrung her hands. "Jack. We need you home."

She looked imploringly at his eyes, but Jack gestured to the camp behind him. "This *is* my home. These are my people, and I was born to lead them and keep everyone safe."

"Aria is lost, and she's alone," Snow said, taking Jack's cool hands. Despite the chill in the air, he did not seem to mind it. "She needs you, Jack."

Jack pulled his hands away as if she had shocked him with an electric eel. "She made her choice," he said, his shoulders squaring and expression hardening. "If she wants to be the villain, I can't change her mind."

"Yes, you can," Snow argued. "In fact, you're the only one who can. But you need to come back with us. That's why we came all this way. You don't know what we've been through. How much we've risked to get here."

Jack raised his palm, and she stopped.

"I'm sorry for your troubles. And I'll give you a safe passage back down," he said with a sigh. "But you wasted your time coming here. I'm not going back. This is who I am and where I belong."

"Don't do this, please," Snow pleaded, shaking her head as tears welled up in her eyes. But Jack's expression was resolute, and the look he gave her was enough to dash a thousand hopes.

"I don't think you're grasping the severity of the situation," Emmett stepped in. "People are suffering under her rule. And despite the strong leader facade that she puts on for others to see, the truth is... she's not happy, Jack."

Snow shot him a curious look, wondering how he knew so much. But Jack appeared unsurprised.

"I know why she's being this way. And I know why you're both here together," Jack said, looking at him so deeply, Emmett took a step back.

"What is he talking about, Emmett? What's going on?" Snow asked, but Emmett avoided her gaze.

Jack looked at her with pity, and it only

stirred up annoyance. "How can you stay away, knowing what she's doing?" Snow hissed, wiping tears from her face as anger took over. "We need you. *She* needs you. How can you just give up on her? I thought you loved her."

"I will *always* love Aria," Jack said firmly. "It's The Snow Queen I cannot condone."

"She's still in there. I know she is. Jack, please…" Snow begged. "Help me bring Aria back."

Jack peered into Snow's eyes, his expression serious. "Aria will not stop until…" He pressed his lips shut as if whatever he knew, it wasn't his place to tell. "You're her target now, and she'll not stop until she's done with you."

Snow gave him a puzzled look. "Me?"

But Jack was done talking. His stare grew cold, and his dark eyes turned white.

"Jack?" Snow said, a sense of unease filling her. Then a gust of wind encircled them, and Snow yelped as she rose up off the ground.

"Goodbye, Snow. Focus on finding your own happy ending and everything will be fine," Jack's steady voice echoed in her ears as she and Emmett clung onto each other.

This is freaky. Put me down. Put me down right now! Knight said through terrified neighs. But despite their pleadings, Jack lifted his hands, and the vortex sent the three of them zooming to the bottom of the mountain.

They landed softly beside the ice bridge and Emmett held onto Knight, panting heavily. "I don't want to ever do that again," he said between breaths. But Snow swiveled on the spot and shook a fist up in the air.

"You coward!" she shouted. "I'll never forgive you for this, you hear me? Never!" She collapsed on her knees, wracked with confusion and grief. Emmett crouched beside her and pulled her in for a tight hug.

"I'm sorry it didn't work out," he said softly. "But at least you tried."

"I failed her," she whispered, her voice trembling.

Emmett lifted her chin, and she could see her devastated face reflected in his clear eyes. "You didn't fail her. *She* failed you. *She* made the choice to be a villain, and *she* made the choice to push Jack away." His gentle eyes softened. "Now, it's time for you to think about *you*. Let's put her behind us and just focus on being happy. Together."

Snow grabbed his face and pressed her lips to his as the thought of building a life with him flooded her mind. They kissed until they ran out of air, then with their foreheads pressed together, Snow opened her eyes.

"Happy. Together." She smiled. "I liked the sound of that."

Emmett sucked in a nervous breath and gave her a serious look. "Then run away with me."

CHAPTER TWELVE

*A*ria stared at the mirror with eyes unblinking. She watched Emmett and her sister, facing one another still at the foot of the Ice Mountains.

Emmett asked Snow to run away with him, and although she hesitated at first, she agreed to go, and they sealed it with a kiss. It almost pained Aria to think that her sister would leave, but Snow deserved to be happy.

The image of Emmett and her sister vanished from the mirror, and Grandfather appeared instead.

"She got it," Aria said, a strange stillness inside her. "My sister got her happy ending.

They're running away after his brother's wedding. It's over."

Aria wanted to be happy for her sister. She finally found her happy ending. Emmett wasn't officially a prince, but he was the prince *charming* she deserved.

"Aria..." Grandfather spoke. He didn't seem happy about the news, but then again, happiness was no longer part of his personality. Every time they would reach a happy ending, he would simply turn a page in his book and move on to the next plan.

Aria was just relieved she didn't have to hurt her sister in any way for her to find true love. Snow's book had to be the easiest so far, and Aria couldn't have been more grateful.

"It's not over yet," Grandfather said in a cold tone.

Aria's brows furrowed. "What do you mean it's not over? He just asked her to run away with him. They can be together without anyone getting in the way. Isn't that what we wanted?"

"That's not the way it should be," he replied.

"Who cares. They're together."

"But it's not true love," he said firmly. "Not yet."

"Maybe not yet, but it will grow."

"Aria…" Grandfather gave her a stern look. "Do you want their relationship to last?"

Aria crossed her arms and went to stand by the window. "Of course I do."

"Then there is more work to be done," he said nonchalantly. "Now, let's keep our focus."

"Easy for you to say," she said, swinging around with a scowl. "It's not you that they hate. This is not even your world."

"But it was the world of the woman I loved," he reminded her. "And it is now the world of my grandson."

"Oh, you want to talk about your grandson?" Aria marched toward the mirror. Good thing that old man was out of her reach, otherwise she would blast him with daggers of ice. "You said I would never lose him. You promised."

"I'm sure he still loves you—"

"He wants nothing to do with me," she said firmly. "You know what he said to me before he left? He said that love isn't something kept in a book. It's a living thing that needs to be nurtured. And I'm starting to think he was right." She turned away from the mirror. "Now, he's never coming back. I've lost him forever."

"Grandfather," the voice of a young man calling out from behind the door of Grandfather's study was too familiar. Aria swung around to face the mirror again. The pressure in her chest was faint but present.

"I'm busy, Jack," Grandfather replied coldly. "I'll be down for supper in a minute."

When Jack didn't respond, Aria bit her lip. She had just seen him with Snow and Emmett at his village, but he looked so different from the young man with brown hair she first met. That boy was behind that door, aching for a love his grandfather never gave him. And it was all her fault.

"How old is he now?" she asked, her voice soft.

Grandfather was silent for a long moment, then he lifted his eyes to meet hers. "He just turned seventeen."

Aria's eyes widened. "That's the age he…"

"Loses me, yes," Grandfather replied, even void of emotion over his own death. "It's only a matter of time before Jack goes through the mirror."

It was hard for Aria to wrap her mind around the time gap between them. She took a seat on the sofa near the mirror, still trying to understand that in Grandfather's timeline, Jack still hadn't gone through the mirror. But yet, in her timeline, he'd lived through so much already. The thoughts of those times flooded her mind. The ogres... the pirates... the *mermaids...*

"Aria..." Grandfather's voice pulled her from her thoughts. "It's important that you don't let your feelings get in the way of doing the right thing."

"Don't worry about me," she said coldly. "I've got it under control."

"This is your sister," he said. "As strong as you may think you are, your heart is a lot more fragile with her than with the others. So for this book, it's best to take things one step at a time. All you need to do is trust me. Look how all the others have worked out so far."

Aria didn't trust anyone, but she couldn't deny that everything he'd told her so far had come true. All the evil she'd done really did

work out for the best. She didn't like the price
she was paying, though. Sacrificing her happiness with Jack was one of the hardest things
she ever had to do. She couldn't just give up
now. Not if it would jeopardize her sister's
happiness. She was so close to getting it.

Her sister.

That echoed in her mind for a long
moment.

"Why didn't you tell me she wasn't my
biological sister?" Aria asked, remembering
what she'd seen through the mirror while her
sister was in the tent.

Grandfather let out a long breath, then
ran a hand through his white hair. "How did
you find out?"

"The mermaids, out of all creatures in this
kingdom…"

"Aria—"

She glared at him. "I had the right to
know!"

"All things must be." He reminded her of
the words of the elves. "It was not my place to
tell you, but it is your place to continue being the
villain of this story. Now, don't lose your focus."

"Just tell me what I need to do next," Aria grunted.

"Right now…" He scanned through the book on his lap. "You need to do whatever it takes to keep that young man from taking your sister away."

"What else?" Aria asked.

"One step at a time, remember? Now, go be a villain." His image vanished from the mirror, and Aria let out a frustrated sigh. He was starting to get on her nerves. But she still needed him. He had the books, and she couldn't restore the happy endings without them.

"Guards!" Aria yelled.

A group of guards barged into her study and took their position by the door. "Yes, My Queen."

"My sister is at the dwarfs' village," she said. "Go get her and bring her home."

The guards exchanged glances with one another. "But, My Queen, wasn't the huntsman supposed to bring her home?"

"Change of plans," Aria said, throwing her cloak over her shoulders. "And when I come back, she better be in her room. Is that clear?"

"Yes, My Queen."

Once the guards left the room, Aria turned to face the mirror again. "Mirror, mirror... show me where I can find that flipping mermaid."

CHAPTER THIRTEEN

Snow fell in and out of sleep as she slumped against Emmett on the back of Knight. Her mind raced with confusing thoughts, and every part of her body ached, longing for a nice bed with goose feather pillows. But leaning back with Emmett's arms around her was the next best thing. By the time Emmett squeezed her arm and woke her up, it was nightfall.

"We're back," he said softly. The orange glow from the lanterns in the street made the quiet houses look peaceful and warm.

Emmett helped Snow get down, and she buried her face in Knight's black mane.

"Thank you so much for your help," she whispered.

Carrying you home has been an honor. Stay safe, sweet princess.

Snow turned to Emmett as he handed her satchel, and suddenly the world grew dim and the clouds hung heavy in the sky. Snow didn't want Emmett to leave.

Emmett brushed her hair away from her face and cradled her head in his strong hands. "I want you to accompany me to my brother's wedding."

"I thought you weren't going to the wedding?" Snow said, her voice soft. "What changed your mind?"

Emmett smiled. "You did."

"Me?" Snow's eyes widened. "How?"

"You don't give up on family, right?"

Warmth filled her heart, and she smiled. "Right."

"So…" Emmett gave her a charming look. "Will you accompany me?"

As much as she wanted to, she couldn't go to the wedding. If Emmett knew what monstrous things she had done, using his brother, she might lose Emmett forever.

"I can't risk it. My sister might be there," she said. But that was a lie. Snow knew Belle would never have invited Aria after all she'd done. But she needed Emmett to stop giving her that pleading look.

"I understand." He offered her a small smile. "After the wedding, I'll ask Nathaniel to grant us safe passage to the Northern realm. Then I will come back for you," he said, his voice vibrating against Snow's ears. She closed her eyes as they pressed their foreheads together.

"Promise?"

Emmett pulled back and gave her a look so sincere, there could not be any doubt.

"I will see you soon."

Snow pulled on the collar of his shirt, urging him to her, and she tasted his lips one last time. His mouth was so soft and tender, and the kiss lasted not nearly as long as she needed. But Emmett pulled away, grasped her hands in his and pressed his lips to the back of her knuckles.

"Farewell, my princess," he said, mounting Knight and giving her a wave.

Snow took fistfuls from her cloth shirt and

watched as Emmett and Knight disappeared into the forest, leaving her all alone.

The next morning, Snow washed the dishes after the dwarfs left for work and lost herself in thought.

Running away with Emmett was the only thing that made sense. Now that she knew she was not a princess, she didn't know who she was. The face of the merman with long, silver hair and ice-blue eyes appeared in her mind once more, and she wondered who the man was. If he was even still alive. Why did he give Snow away? And who was her real mother?

Roger flew across the sky and Snow watched him, wondering how simple her life would have been if she were an owl.

"Hello, Roger. I haven't seen you for days!" she said, delighted as Roger swooped in and landed on the windowsill. Usually, he would fly to his favorite tree and get ready to sleep the day away. But today, he ruffled his feathers and hopped side to side like he was walking on a bed of coals. Snow frowned. "What's the matter?"

It's Belle's father. Snow's heart pinched at the alarm in his voice. She bit her lip, cursing herself for letting the man leave the alley.

"Oh Roger. Don't tell me he's…"

He's alive, Roger said quickly. *And he's going to do something terrible at the wedding.*

Snow opened her mouth and closed it again, reeling at the news. Belle and Nathaniel's royal wedding was today. A rush of adrenaline coursed through Snow, and her heart thumped in her chest as Roger flew in and fanned her with his wings.

Come on. We have to leave right now. I'll tell you everything on the way.

"All right. But wait…" Snow threw the apron off and tossed it on the counter, then hurried to a little wardrobe with her dresses hanging in it.

Snow, we don't have much time, Roger warned as Snow looked through the dresses.

"Just wait. If I'm going to a royal wedding… I need to make sure I look the part."

*T*he dwarfs lent Snow their donkey named Filo. He was not the fastest method of transport, but they crossed the forest much faster than if Snow had been on foot.

The sun beamed gloriously over the palace, and the sandstone blinded Snow as she approached. A vast line of fine carriages sat outside the gates, waiting for the guards to inspect them.

They'll never let you in on a donkey, Roger said, flying overhead.

Hey! What is that supposed to mean? Filo said with a grunt. *Am I not noble enough for a royal wedding?* Snow shushed him and tickled his ears.

"Wait here. I'm going to walk," she said to the donkey, who started munching on some apples on the ground. Meanwhile, Roger flew ahead.

I'll find Emmett, he called back before he disappeared over the palace wall.

Snow got down and smoothed out her thick cotton dress that poofed out thanks to the netting she fashioned into an underskirt. The blue dress was simple, but she was clean and fixed her hair to sit in an elaborate braid wrapped around the back of her head.

She then pinched her cheeks to make them rosy and combed her lips with her teeth to make them plumper. It was the best she could do.

Roger returned and settled on her outstretched arm. *I found him. He's inside but he saw me. He's coming out now.*

Snow's heart fluttered at the thought of seeing Emmett. Probably all dressed up in formal clothes and looking like the dashing prince that he is.

When Emmett came into view, Snow was not disappointed by what she saw. His dark hair was carefully combed to the side and his beard short, neatly trimmed. But nothing could take Snow's eyes off his broad grin.

"I'm so happy you changed your mind!" he said, rushing toward her. "You look beautiful!" He picked her up and spun her around in a circle before putting her down and kissing her cheek.

"I need to tell you something," Snow said,

feeling out of breath as Emmett took her hand and rested it in the crook of his arm. But he was in too good of a mood to notice.

"I hope you've brought your appetite," he said as they walked right past the guards and into the palace grounds. "There's enough food to feed an army."

Snow swallowed nervously as she took in the vast displays. Red roses flooded the gardens and ivory lace hung in waves along the trees. In the courtyard, a string orchestra played romantic music, and the buzz of excited chatter had Snow's heart speeding.

"Everything looks beautiful," she said. Then snapping out of her daze, she grabbed Emmett's arm and forced him to stop walking and look at her. "Belle's father is here. And he's going to poison your brother. We have to stop him."

Emmett's eyes stretched wide. "How do you know that?"

"Roger told me." Snow kept her voice low as a couple walked by.

Emmett puffed the air from his cheeks. "So, a little bird told you?"

"Yes," Snow said. "And I believe him

because… Belle's father is Rumpelstiltskin. And he is dangerous. I saw him kill a man with my own eyes."

Emmett blinked several times, and Snow reasoned he must have been in shock. But there was no time for him to recover. "Come on, we have to——"

A deep cough stopped her in her tracks. She sucked in the air through her teeth at a strong grip around her arm.

"Guard, get your hands off this lady at once," Emmett ordered, pulling out his silver sword. Two more guards stepped in with their swords drawn and looked at Emmett.

"I'm sorry, sir. But we have strict orders to keep her away from the palace," the guard said.

"Orders from whom?" Emmett asked, keeping his sword drawn.

"Emmett, please…" Snow pleaded with a guard on each side, but Emmett didn't listen.

"Orders from *whom*?" he asked again, but with a tone a lot more threatening than before.

"King Nathaniel, sir."

Emmett stared at the guard as if he'd slapped him. "What?"

"Emmett, you cannot be escorted out, too," Snow begged. "Now, please, put the sword away."

Emmett took in a deep breath, then sheathed his sword. "Where will you be taking her?"

"The Snow Queen has ordered that she be taken back to the palace at once."

Snow's heart sank at the white and silver armored guards waiting at the gate. But then she shook her head and looked at Emmett again. "It's okay. My sister won't hurt me. You need to go and… save him."

Emmett tried to argue but the guards secured their grip on Snow and frog-marched her away. Snow looked back at Emmett, who staggered forward as if to attack them from behind, but she shook her head.

She turned away with Emmett's look of devastation burning in her mind.

CHAPTER FOURTEEN

*E*mmet hurried into the castle with his hands balled into tight fists. He stomped down the hall and headed toward the main ballroom, hardly taking in the lords and ladies milling around him. After the ceremony, the guests probably headed to the banquet. Then his brother was most likely going to say a few words to his bride and invite everyone for a toast.

Emmett picked up the pace and started running. If anyone thought for one second that they could come into his kingdom and threaten to kill his family, they were gravely mistaken. Even if his brother was a beast.

He burst through the double doors, only to find Belle in an elegant white gown dancing, the huge skirt embroidered with white roses. She was with her father in the center of the ballroom, looking adoringly into his eyes as though she was savoring every moment she had with him. Guests stood in a circle, watching them waltz.

Emmett scanned the room for his brother. He was sitting across the way, watching Belle like she was a beautiful sunset. But there were no drinks on their table and a wave of relief washed over Emmett. Maybe he wasn't too late.

Emmett wiped the beads of sweat from his forehead with the back of his hand, then made his way toward his brother's table. He just needed to make sure Nathaniel didn't drink anything unless it came from a newly stoppered bottle and served right before his eyes. He would make his brother dehydrated on his wedding day if necessary.

Nathaniel grinned as he approached his bride on the dance floor. He bowed to her father, then waited. Belle's father gave her a kiss on the cheek, then gave Nathaniel a bow of approval before stepping aside. Emmett gritted his teeth. The nerve the old man had to be so courteous in front of his daughter, all the while planning to murder the king. He was going to be dragged out of the kingdom with his ankles tied to four angry stallions. Emmett would make sure of that, if it was the last thing he did before leaving for good.

Once Nathaniel took up a waltz with his bride, Belle's father backed away from the dance floor. With everyone's eyes trained on the newlyweds, Emmett was the only one who saw him dart out the door toward the hallway. Emmett hurried after him, weaving through the crowd watching the couple dance.

Just as Emmett stepped out into the hall-way, he caught sight of Belle's father rounding the corner. He ran down the hall, eager to catch up, but after every corner, he would catch only a glimpse of Belle's father's back. Until he finally caught him entering the library.

Emmett stopped by the door and pulled out his silver sword before entering the room.

"That's a little much, don't you think?" The man's voice came from the corner of the room. Emmett turned to his left with his weapon in hand. Belle's father sat on the sofa with his legs crossed and his arm resting over the back cushion.

"What are you doing here?" Emmett hissed.

"Waiting for you," Belle's father said, glancing at Emmett's sword unfazed. "After all, if you're planning to kill me, I didn't want it done in front of my baby girl."

Emmett tightened his grip on the hilt of his sword. "And killing your baby girl's husband doesn't bother you?"

Belle's father arched a surprised brow. "You think I want to kill the king?"

"I know about your plan to poison him," Emmett spoke through gritted teeth. "I also know you're Rumpelstiltskin."

Belle's father smiled. "Well, that's only a minor detail."

"Your plan has failed," Emmett aimed his sword at Rumpel. "And now I will kill you myself to make sure you never hurt anyone."

"First of all, if you kill me, you will

become the new Rumpelstiltskin. I don't think your little princess would enjoy that as much. And second…" He rose to his feet and pulled something out of his pocket. "I didn't come to poison the king. I came to give you a gift."

He held up a vial of blue liquid.

"What is that?" Emmett asked.

"It's not poison, if that's what you're thinking. It's a cure," he said, placing it on a small table between them. "He drinks that and the beast inside of him will be gone. He will be fully human again."

Emmett lowered his weapon and stared at the vial. "How do I know if you're telling the truth?"

"You don't," he said with a shrug. "But if there's anyone I love more than my own life, it's my sweet Belle. All I want is for her to be safe. And for as long as that beast still lives inside of him, she will not be safe."

"Nathaniel would never hurt Belle," Emmett assured him.

"I'm sure the wolf that killed your parents must've cried himself to sleep, but that doesn't change the outcome, does it?" Rumpel gave him a serious look. "The beast, in particular, was mind-controlled, which means he's unstable."

"That was Prince John's doing. But he's dead now."

"It wasn't just Prince John who used the beast for their own gain," Rumpel said with a cunning smile. "Seems like your little sweet princess hasn't told you everything."

Emmett raised his sword again. "Snow would never have manipulated someone like that."

Rumpel raised his hands in mock surrender. "I see you haven't been told half of it. Either way, I did not come here for this. I came as a father. Now, I'm sure you want your brother back just as much as I want to keep my Belle safe. Am I wrong?"

Emmett didn't have to respond. Him leaving his kingdom and his brother behind said it all.

"Very well, then." Rumpel smiled. "You have until the toast to make a choice. If you choose not to do it, then be prepared to reap the consequences."

"I am not going to stand here and allow you to threaten me."

"It's not a threat. It's a fact," he said, holding up a finger. "A subtle difference, but an important one, nonetheless." He strode over to Emmett. "Every choice has consequences. Take me, for example." He opened his arms wide as if displaying himself. "How do you think I became Rumpelstiltskin?"

Emmett didn't bother responding.

Rumpel let out a chuckle. "My precious Belle wished on a wild dandelion, and I paid the price. Before I knew it, I was waking up from a blackout, standing over the old Rumpel's dead body. Now, don't get me wrong. I am not angry with her. After all, that's just being a parent. But it doesn't change the ripple effect that our choices have on those around us."

"What consequences are we talking about?" Emmett asked, his jaw clenched.

"If you choose not to protect my Belle, then someone you love will pay the price."

Emmett raised his sword again. "You stay away from Snow!"

Why he thought about her at the first utterance of the word *love*, Emmett wasn't entirely sure. But the thought of any harm coming to her just about drove him mad.

"Oh, no need to worry about her," Rumpel said, waving it off. "The Snow Queen and I are on good terms at the moment."

Emmett stepped forward with his sword drawn. "Then who will suffer the consequences if I don't follow through?"

Rumpel dropped his hands and gave Emmett a stern look. "It doesn't matter because curing your brother is everything you've ever wanted. Or do I stand corrected?"

Emmett's chest deflated. He hated that Rumpel wasn't wrong.

"I believe the banquet is about to start," Rumpel said, grabbing the vial from the table and tossing it to Emmett. He caught it in midair, then stared at the blue liquid with a mixture of guilt and pleasure.

He did want his brother back.

Rumpel smiled. "Shall we?"

During dinner, while all the guests enjoyed their food, Emmett approached the king and queen's table, holding two glasses of champagne. Belle rose and gave Emmett a hug. They've always had a love-hate relationship. He would tease her, and she would scowl at him. Though, at the moment, she didn't seem as cold with him as other times. Perhaps, entering into the family made her decide to start with a clean slate. Or it could be that she was too happy to let anyone, including him, ruin her joyful moment.

"I always knew," he whispered, giving her a teasing look.

"Knew what?" she asked, raising a brow.

"That you found me attractive." He flashed her a smile. "You just happened to find a nicer version of me."

Belle put a hand on her waist and narrowed her eyes at him. "I see your time in the wild hasn't changed you a bit."

"Just try not to think of me on your wedding night, okay?" He winked, then chuckled when she rolled her eyes.

By the time Emmett turned to face his twin brother, he was already standing with a broad grin on his face. "I'm so happy you're here!" Nathaniel gave his brother a firm hug. "But you throw your charms at my queen again, and I will claw your eyes out."

Emmett laughed. And by the smile in his brother's face when he pulled back, he knew that he missed the banter between them too.

"Here." Emmett offered him one of the drinks. "I would like to make a toast, if I may?" Nathaniel's grin grew wider, and he took the glass with pride.

Emmett made his way to the center of the ballroom where the couple had danced and raised a glass. "May I have everyone's attention, please." Once everyone's eyes were on him, he turned to face the king and queen. "I would like to say a few words to the happy couple."

Marian's eyes filled with tears as she sat next to Robin at a table near her brother's.

"As many of you may know, my brother and I have had our differences, as I'm sure all families do," Emmett began. "But it's the similarities we share that keep me from giving up on him. And though I've tried to stay away, I see him everywhere I go. I mean, I do have his face."

The guests laughed, as did Nathaniel and Belle.

"The truth is, I walked away because there were things about him I could not accept. But none of that will matter after tonight because I've returned, determined to get my brother back. And to ask that he forgive me for all of my bad decisions. Past, present, and… future." Emmett raised his glass, as did everyone else, including Nathaniel. "To new beginnings."

"To new beginnings!" the guests echoed.

Emmett drank his glass, then watched as his brother downed his drink. Belle took a sip of hers, just enough to wet her lips, then turned to Nathaniel to steal a kiss.

When the orchestra began to play, Nathaniel pulled Belle to her feet and accompanied her to the dance floor. Emmett moved out of the way but watched the happy couple starting another waltz. More couples began joining the king and queen and danced around them.

"I see you've made your choice," Rumpel's

voice came from behind him. Emmett shoved a hand into his pocket and traced the cork of the vial that hadn't been opened. Rumpel appeared at his side, and Emmett's heart raced with nerves.

"He won't hurt her," Emmett assured him.

"You've been warned." By the time Emmett turned, Rumpel was gone. He scanned around the room, but he was nowhere in sight.

As soon as he caught his brother and Belle sneaking out to the patio, he hurried after them. "Nathaniel, wait!"

Nathaniel swung around with Belle on his arm. "Is something wrong?"

"Yes." Emmett took the vial from his pocket and handed it to Nathaniel. "Belle's father wanted me to put this in your drink. It's a cure for—"

"I know what it is," Nathaniel said, taking the vial and staring at the blue liquid.

Belle stared at it with a horrified expression. "Why would my father want that?"

"You might want to have a chat with him," Emmett replied. "It might not have worked tonight, but he seemed determined, so... be careful."

"Why didn't you?" Nathaniel asked, looking up from the vial to meet his brother's eyes. "Why didn't you give it to me?"

He thought about Snow and what she'd said once. Her sister had repeated the same words at one point, and it was the only thing echoing in his mind. "We don't give up on family."

Nathaniel pulled Emmett into another hug, clapping him on the back.

"How did you find out?" Belle asked, her face downcast. Whether she knew what her father had become, and that it had been her fault, Emmett wasn't sure. But she seemed guilty.

"Snow warned me," he said.

Belle looked at Emmett, shocked. "Snow? Aria's sister?"

Emmett nodded. "Yes. She was here earlier but was rudely escorted off of the premises."

Belle shared a glance with Nathaniel, then the both of them lowered their eyes to the floor.

"It was her, wasn't it?" Emmett said, reading their obvious expression. "She was the one manipulating you after Prince John lost the mermaid stone."

When neither of them responded, or even bothered looking Emmett in the eyes, he knew. "If you'll excuse me. I have to go."

"Where to?" Nathaniel asked.

Emmett squared his shoulders. "Get answers."

CHAPTER FIFTEEN

Snow hugged her knees as she sat on the window ledge of her old room, looking out at the quiet castle grounds. Two guards stood outside her door while Aria was away. So, Snow was locked up in a very pretty cell until Aria returned.

The night's sky was clear over the castle, and she could make out thousands of stars twinkling like jewels. She shut her eyes, breathing in the cool air and allowing her imagination to run wild.

She pictured Emmett storming through the wedding, boldly saving his brother from imminent death and exposing Belle's father as the new Rumpelstiltskin. She gritted her teeth with a hiss as an image of Belle's father flooded her mind.

Rumpelstiltskin had a formidable reputation for being cruel, clever, conniving, and the most powerful man in all the kingdoms. No one knew how or why, but it was rumored that he had the ability to spin cotton into gold and convince unsuspecting victims to enter into a contract that would only end in misery. He was not someone she wanted to make an enemy.

Snow shuddered against the thought and buried her face in her dress. The sooner Emmett came for her, the sooner they could run away to the Northern Realm and start a new life together.

Snow longed for a fresh start. Where no one knew who she was or what terrible things she had done. The Northern Realm was seldom talked about. The mermaid-infested waters made it dangerous for sailors to cross unless a deal was made with Poseidon, King of the Seas.

Snow's breath hitched as she remembered that she was half mermaid. Perhaps the Northern Realm would hold the key to finding out who she really was. Maybe she and Emmett could work together to find out more about her family.

The sound of horses' hooves approaching the castle pulled Snow from her thoughts and she snapped her eyes open.

"Emmett!" she whispered, watching the prince ride his steed up to the castle. He dismounted his horse and looked up at her. But his face was in the shadows and she couldn't see his expression. She hoped he would be grinning. That would mean he saved his brother and all was well.

Snow couldn't contain her excitement. She climbed out the window and lowered herself until she hung from the ledge. Grabbing a vine, she climbed down to meet him. She could have escaped sooner, but she was too tired to run from her sister. Besides, she knew Emmett would come for her at The Snow Queen's palace, and she was right. As soon as her feet hit the ground, she spun around and threw her arms around Emmett's neck.

His shoulders tensed, and he tore her hands from him.

"What's wrong?" Snow asked, then

gasped, covering her mouth with a hand. "Is your brother okay? Did you stop Rumpel from..."

"He's fine," Emmett cut in, his voice cold as ice. Snow hugged herself, taken over by the chill in the space between them.

"I'm glad," she said, her voice weakening. Something was horribly wrong, and with the way Emmett stared at her, his face hard and jaw jutting out, she could only think of one reason why.

Belle and Nathaniel must've told him the truth. Snow bit her lip as her eyes brimmed with tears. He didn't need to say it. They told him everything, she knew it.

"Tell me it's not true," Emmett said, his voice breaking. For a split second, his hardened expression gave way to sadness. It wasn't a demand. It was a plea.

Snow wanted so badly for it not to have been true that it made her heart ache. She wanted to tell him that it was all just a big misunderstanding and that Belle and Nathaniel were wrong about her. But none of that was true. And under his stare, Snow couldn't bring herself to lie.

Emmett took a step back, shaking his head. "No…" he said barely above a whisper. His reaction sent a jolt straight through Snow's chest and she cried softly, the flood gates opening. Before she knew it, all of her thoughts came spilling out.

"I had to do something," she said, pressing her fingernails into her arms as she held herself tighter. It was as though her whole body was breaking apart and this was the only way she was keeping herself in one piece as her heart splintered, threatening to shatter at any moment. "Aria had to be stopped. So, when I found out that Prince John was using Nathaniel to terrorize the villages with the mermaid stone, I had Roger steal it from him."

She stopped to take a breath and studied Emmett's face for any sign of forgiveness, or at least understanding. But there was nothing but coldness as he stood immobile, waiting for her to continue. Snow shut her eyes to steal some courage.

"It's true. I used the mermaid stone to control your brother." She opened her eyes and took a step closer. "But he never hurt anyone under my control," she added. "I've only ever used him to look for the genie bracelet so I could put it on my sister. It was the only way to keep her from using her powers." Snow reached out for Emmett's hand, but he stepped away.

"You think that makes it all right? To take away someone's will?" The incredulity in his voice sliced through Snow's heart and it throbbed, bleeding into her chest and flooding her with emotion.

"I'm sorry. I'm so sorry, I was just so focused on trying to stop Aria, I didn't think—"

"You're right," Emmett interjected, his voice landing on her like a lightning bolt. "You didn't think about anyone but yourself. You keep saying you did it to stop Aria from hurting others, but I know why you really did it."

Snow lifted her gaze to stare at Emmett in horror.

He leaned forward and spoke with a deathly whisper. "Revenge for your beloved George."

His name was the final blow to her heart,

and Snow fell to the ground, her body wracked with grief and shame as she sobbed. "I'm so sorry."

Emmett cleared his throat and Snow wiped her eyes furiously, blinking and daring to hope that he might say something to make her feel less wretched. But his eyes were cast upward.

"My Queen," he shouted.

Snow frowned and craned her neck to see Aria standing at the balcony over her room.

"We made a deal," he continued. "Now, I want my safe passage to the Northern Realm."

Aria took a parchment from her cloak, then used a tiny swirl of wind to lower it down until it landed on Emmett's hand.

Snow's mouth dropped. "You were working for *her*? All this time?"

Emmett's jaw hardened and he barely looked at her. "Goodbye, Snow."

The words were colder than the harshest winter, and he turned and walked away, leaving Snow to crumble, her heart breaking into a million pieces as she drenched the ground with her tears.

CHAPTER SIXTEEN

*A*ria paced her study, wringing her hands and biting back tears. "Mirror, Mirror… show me Grandfather."

She stopped, listening to the faint sobs coming from the next room. Snow had cried herself to sleep, and now she was crying again, and it made Aria want to break something.

When the old man appeared in the mirror, Aria couldn't bring herself to even look at him. "I did everything you told me to do. Now, Emmett has gone and my sister is heartbroken."

She stole a glance and anger brewed inside her chest at the nonchalant look Grandfather gave her.

"You're not seriously telling me this was part of the plan?" she asked incredulously.

"A union born from lies would never last," Grandfather said with a simple shrug.

Aria frowned so deeply, her vision blurred. "I'm sick of your cryptic lines, old man."

"Aria." And for the first time, Grandfather's voice was soft. She stopped pacing and looked at him, waiting.

"Now it is time to make amends with your sister," he said. The words hit Aria square between the eyes.

"Amends?" Aria echoed. "She wants nothing to do with me. And honestly, I can't blame her. Everything I've done has made her life miserable." Aria balled her fists, resisting the urge to blast daggers of ice through the mirror.

"Take her for a walk in the garden," he said. "And tell her the truth."

Aria's fists unclenched and her breath hitched. "You mean it? I can tell her... everything?"

Grandfather nodded. "Everything," he said. But then he dipped his head and peered at her with so much intensity, Aria stepped back. "You just need to do one last thing, and your role in Snow's story will be complete."

---

*A*ria swallowed nervously, then ran her fingers through her hair as she waited for her sister next to the lake. She had washed up and put on her finest white gown. The sleeves came to her wrists, and its lace overlay had been handsewn by the maids. It was a symbol of *hope* that the past could be washed clean, and she and Snow could move on and start anew.

She looked around the spring garden and raised her palm, shooting blasts of ice, then curling her fingers as she manipulated them to form powdery snow, covering the grounds in white. Snow always loved winter. Perhaps it would help her to feel more at ease. As she looked at their own private winter garden, the corners of her mouth picked up. The cold was fresh and invigorating, and it was the perfect setting. For there was nothing as pure as snow.

She looked up at the sound of approaching footsteps and watched her guard accompany Snow White into the garden. Aria smiled with approval at the sight of her. The maids had powdered her face, removing any traces of dark circles under her eyes or her tear stains. And her black hair sat in soft waves to her shoulders.

She wore a simple dress with a red tie at the waist, and for a moment Aria was reminded of days long past.

"I'm so glad you came," Aria said, keeping her voice soft as Snow reached her. But Snow's eyes darkened, and she placed her hands on her hips as the guard left them.

"I didn't know I had a choice."

Aria tried not to let her feelings show as Snow's retort hit her. "I know you hate me, and maybe you always will. But before you give up on me, I want to tell you everything."

"... So the only way for us to get our happy ending is if there's a villain?" Snow asked as they walked around the lake. They stopped near a tree, and Snow sat on the little bench, her eyes wide as she looked at the ground. Aria had told her all that Grandfather had said. About Jack's world, and the books. That Grandfather was The Intruder who came through the mirror many years ago and messed with everyone's happy endings. And how he asked for Aria's help to fix his mistake. Since The Evil Queen was dead, Aria took her place as the villain.

"Snow. Playing this role has been nothing short of torture," Aria said. The burden of her actions laid heavy on her chest and exhaustion overwhelmed her whole body. Snow frowned at her, but Aria picked up a flash of sympathy in her eyes.

"But how could you?" Snow asked. "Red was your best friend. Robin took you in when you had no one. Belle has never done anything but help you. And you betrayed all of them."

"I know." Aria looked away, her heart heavy as a rock. "And had I not done what I did, I would not have been strong enough to fulfill my role."

Snow narrowed her eyes. "What did you do?"

Aria turned to meet her sister's eyes.

"Before my coronation," she said, "I froze my own heart."

Snow gasped. "You did what?"

Aria touched her chest, remembering the day she congealed her heart in order to fully emerge into The Snow Queen. How she placed a hand over it and clenched her jaw, letting the ice cold spread through her skin and encase her throbbing heart. The change was instantaneous. The coldness spread, numbing her sensations and feelings. It was surprisingly refreshing. Her tears stopped and her mind was clearer than it had ever been. "If I hadn't done so, I would never have been able to follow through with any of it."

Snow covered her mouth in surprise. "Now it makes sense why you threw George off the balcony without any hesitation," Snow muttered. "But why did you do it?"

Aria frowned. "He was a threat to our kingdom."

"But I loved him, Aria."

It didn't go unnoticed how Snow said *loved*, as in past tense. But she didn't call her sister out on it. "I discovered something about him," Aria said. "Something that would not have made you happy. Besides, Emmett is your true love."

"But he's not," Snow argued, rising to her feet and her cheeks flushing red. "He's gone, and none of that was real. He was just doing his job to keep me safe. He lied to me."

If Aria's heart hadn't been frozen, she would have been in tears at that moment. "Out of all the horrible things I've done, hurting *you* has by far been the hardest thing I've ever had to do." She sat on the bench and held out her arms. Snow's frown deepened, but then her eyes grew glassy and she fell into Aria's arms.

"I hate that I can't stay mad at you," Snow cried. "No matter how much I want to, I can't."

Aria stroked Snow's soft hair and shushed her. "I've missed you so much," Aria said, wiping the tears streaming down her sister's face.

The two sisters sat, comforting each other for a long time. Then Aria looked up at the fruit hanging from the tree above their heads.

"Here," she said, plucking a juicy red apple and offering it to Snow. "Call it a peace offering. I promise I will never meddle in your life again."

Snow wiped her wet cheeks and took the apple with an appreciative chuckle. "I'm going to hold you to that." Then she studied the apple.

"I was too upset to eat breakfast, but this looks delicious now."

Aria beamed as Snow bit into the apple, and for a moment they sat there, eyes locked and wearing identical smiles. But then Snow's face fell, and she dropped the apple on the ground. Aria's eyes widened in horror as she watched her sister fall back. She leaped forward and grabbed Snow just before she hit the ground, and held her in her arms.

"Snow? Snow!" Aria shouted as her sister's eyes fluttered closed. "Snow!" Her breath quickened as she shook her sister. Snow lay in her arms, her pretty eyes closed and face white as a ghost.

When she didn't wake, Aria looked at the bitten apple lying a few feet away and remembered what Grandfather told her. *"Be sure to give her an apple from the tree in the garden as a token of your fresh start."* Aria looked at the tree standing so close to the Lake of Reason, and her heart throbbed in her chest for the first time in months.

"No..." she whispered with horror. "No, no, no, no."

Being unable to wake her sister when they had just made amends was enough to melt the ice around her heart, and the rush of pain was so sudden that it took her breath away. She shook her head, tears falling freely. She clung onto Snow's body as grief wracked through her whole being. Every inch of her splintered in pain, and her heart stung so deeply, she thought the grief might destroy her completely.

"Snow, wake up, Snow!"

With one final look at Snow's lifeless body, Aria let out an unearthly scream so powerful, it sent a massive shockwave through the whole garden and out to the rest of the kingdom. The snow turned to ice, frozen fractals formed in the trees, and all was frozen for as far as the eye could see.

Guards rushed out in a panic, slipping on the ice as they approached. Aria allowed them to take Snow's body. "Take her to the throne room," she said, her voice shaking. She stood, her legs barely able to carry her. But anger propelled her forward.

Aria staggered up the stairs, then waved her hand, blasting ice against the double doors of the study, bursting them open. She stomped angrily toward the mirror with her head thumping and a dreadful hollowness in her midriff. She clutched her stomach as she gritted her teeth. "Mirror, Mirror, show me Grandfather, now!"

Grandfather appeared but did not even raise a brow at her sorry state.

"I should've killed you when I had the chance, you lying, evil old man," Aria hissed. "You never told me the apple was poisoned, and now she's dead. My sister is—"

"She's not dead," Grandfather said simply. "She's merely asleep in your world and has awoken in mine."

"What?" Aria looked at the old man as if he'd slapped her. "How is she there?"

"The tree from which you took the apple has its roots watered by the Lake of Reason, which means the moment your sister bit into the fruit, she woke up here. In my world."

Aria balled her fists. "How do I bring her back?'

Grandfather smiled. "You don't. Only true love's kiss will."

Aria's mind raced and her whole body ached. She glanced out the window and looked out at the frozen kingdom. The shockwave she sent had put them into an eternal winter, and she had no idea how to reverse it.

"But how will that happen if Emmett is gone?"

"Here is what you do next—" The sound of a grunt caught Aria's attention and she swung around. The old man's eyes and mouth were wide open and it didn't look like he was breathing.

"Grandfather!" She rushed toward the mirror as he choked. But when he stepped back, Aria gasped at the sight of a sword sticking out from his chest. A pool of blood began to grow and stain his shirt. Her stomach lurched as she watched the lights fade from his eyes.

"Grandfather, no!" she screeched, trying to reach the mirror. He hadn't told her what to do next. How to save her sister without

Emmett. Then a hand appeared on the old man's shoulder and pushed his body aside.

Aria staggered back, clutching her stomach and panting as a familiar face appeared. He had a rat-like pointy nose, a sloping grin and straw-like hair as he sneered at her. The blood drained from Aria's face as she looked at the man with recognition.

"George?" She blinked several times as her brain scrambled to make sense of what she was seeing as he pushed himself right through the mirror and back into their world. His inky black eyes bore into her soul, and he gave her a smile so wicked, the hairs on the back of Aria's neck stood on end.

"Hello, old friend."

CHAPTER SEVENTEEN

*E*mmett leaned over the wooden railing of a sailor's ship and gazed into the horizon. He tightened his cloak as the frigid chill blew through the harbor. Though Emmett had a feeling that even if the weather warmed, the cold inside him wouldn't fade any time soon.

If only they would just take off already. The sooner he moved on to his new life, the sooner he could put everything behind him. Though he didn't get to say goodbye to his brother, he did stop by Sherwood on his way to the harbor and spoke with his sister. He didn't stay long. Mainly because memories of

Snow began to flood his mind. The wagon, the lobster, the lake. Everywhere he looked in the Chanted Forest reminded him of Snow. And memories of her made his heart ache.

Emmett wasn't a stranger to pain. He'd lost his parents, and for some time, he believed both of his siblings had also been killed. But somehow, the pain that struck him the moment he walked away from Snow surpassed all of it. He'd lived alone in a castle which had once buzzed with life and joy, but yet nothing had made him so empty and cold as he did without her.

He wasn't angry at her because she wanted revenge. Emmett was familiar with the poisonous feeling himself. After all, he'd killed more wolves than he could count because he was also blinded by vengeance. So much so, when he heard about a beast on the loose, he himself had searched for the creature with the intent of piercing him with his silver sword. And when he couldn't catch it, he started a campaign for all hunters to go on a killing spree. What if he had killed his own brother? It would've been all her fault. She was the one controlling him and making him terrify the villages.

The beast was hated and feared in the whole kingdom, which meant that if the people ever found out the truth about his brother, there could be an uprising. And it wasn't even his brother's fault. He never wanted to harm anyone or to terrorize the people. Nathaniel was the kindest person Emmett had ever known. Even when they were little and their father took them hunting, Nathaniel always missed the target on purpose because he couldn't bear to kill an animal. He didn't mind eating them once they cooked, but getting his hands dirty was never his strength.

Emmett could not even imagine the night-mares his brother had to endure. The memories that plagued his mind from all the atrocious acts he was forced to do. And did it all against his will. It was unforgivable.

But then Snow's beautiful face would surface from the back of his mind and all the hate would turn into pain. The image of her pleading for him not to go. The shock of having found out the truth about his deal with her sister. The sound of her shattered cries as he walked away. It was unbearable. His heart was like an anvil in his chest, and it ached as if he'd been pierced with a dagger that he couldn't pull out.

The sound of an explosion erupted in the distance, and Emmett swung around just as a blizzard rushed in his direction like a tsunami. The sailors stopped and watched the phenomenon with eyes unblinking. The violent winds hit the crew with such an immense force, it threw them to the wooden deck.

Emmett was thrown off the boat, but instead of splashing into the water, his back hit an icy ground. He pushed himself to his knees, watching as the blizzard froze the ocean as far as the eye could see.

Then he caught a movement in the sky. Roger flew in circles high above Emmett's head. The sound he was making was unlike anything Emmett had ever heard. It wasn't just louder than usual, it was panicked like an alarm call.

Emmett stretched out his arm, and Roger swooped down and landed on Emmett's fore-arm. But he didn't stay still. He kept flapping his wings and hooting like he was crying. Maybe even sobbing. Though Emmett couldn't understand what he was saying, he knew exactly what message Roger was trying to convey.

Snow was in trouble.

CHAPTER EIGHTEEN

*A*ria woke up with a maddening headache. She raised her hand to her temple and felt her throbbing pulse beat against her fingertips. It took several moments for her to work out where she was. She looked at the mirror, which had broken into fragments, barely kept together. Huge cracks appeared between the shards, and Aria wondered if it even worked anymore.

George had escaped and he was stronger than ever.

She gulped at the memory. Jack's grandfather didn't die of natural causes like Jack had thought. He was *murdered*. And by George. She shut her eyes and took several deep breaths to steady herself. How did George even end up in Grandfather's timeline? When Grandfather went back to his realm in Oxford, he didn't just cross worlds, he also went back in *time*. Back to when Jack was a baby. Maybe when she pushed George through the portal, he went to the same place and time as Grandfather did because he was the last person to go through the mirror. That was the only reasoning Aria's brain could come up with at that moment.

Her chest tightened at the thought that it was her fault that Grandfather was murdered. If she hadn't thrown George to Oxford, Grandfather would never have died. How could she ever tell Jack that?

Jack!

Grandfather never got to tell Jack about the mirror. She rushed toward the mirror, unable to stop the tears falling from her face.

"Mirror…" she shouted in panic. "Show me Jack in Oxford."

The mirror changed from her reflection to that of a graveyard. A mass of people huddled around an open grave. Aria sniffed as she looked through all the faces. Then her eyes landed on a young man with muddy brown hair, wearing a dark suit and throwing a rose into the grave.

"Goodbye, Grandfather," Jack whispered above the grave. When his eyes lifted, Aria held her breath. The young man's eyes locked with hers and they stretched wide with surprise. Aria watched him, her body tingling as if an invisible cord tethered them together, and she felt strength coursing through her veins.

It was Jack, but before he came through the mirror. Aria longed to reach in and pull him in for a tight hug. But then he faded, and the mirror brought her reflection back into view.

"No!" Aria said, edging closer. "Mirror, Mirror, show me Jack in Oxford again," she said, barely breathing. Suddenly, she could see Grandfather's office again, but this time no one was in it. "Jack?" She raised a palm and a flash of cold air shot from her hand, cracking open the study door with a squeal. Aria looked at her palm with surprise. She had never done that before.

A movement by the door caught her attention and she looked up. She bit her lip, seeing Jack walk in. He looked around the study, then placed a finger on an open book and read for a moment. Aria watched, her heart melting and twisting at the sight of him. "Jack, I need you," she whispered as she raised her palm. Another blast shot from her palm, and he jumped back. His brown eyes lifted and met hers for a moment. They stretched wide and he edged closer. But he stopped. Aria gritted her teeth. With the state of the mirror, it could hardly hold together or let him see her fully. But she needed him to try.

"Jack, I need you," she whispered again. But he seemed not able to hear her. She set her jaw and focused on Jack, raising her hand. She blasted another wind and directed it to bend and hit Jack from behind. He stumbled, grabbed the edge of the mirror, then fell forward. The mirror shattered into a million pieces, covering the whole study like glitter.

Aria stood panting, blinking at the empty space where the mirror once was. She looked around her, wondering if she might see Jack. But she was entirely alone.

Aria shut her eyes as they filled with endless tears, and she clenched her fists. Her emotions were amplifying her powers, and if she didn't get them under control, she would never be able to help Snow.

The door opened with a bang and Aria turned just as Emmett rushed in. "Where is she?" he demanded. "Where is Snow?"

Before Aria could say anything, a guard came in. "Your Majesty. George has been here, and he's taken Snow White."

Emmett looked at the guard with incredulity. "George?" He turned to Aria. "Surely not Prince George?"

Aria inclined her head and looked out the window. Snowflakes fell like ash from the gray skies. A white barn owl swooshed inside and hooted, flying around Aria's head. "Do you know where he's taken her?" Aria asked the bird, recognizing it to be Roger. Though she couldn't understand the bird's reply, he hooted and flew out the door before coming back in.

"He knows," Emmett assured her.

"Then let's go!" Aria rushed down the stairs, picking up a satchel on her way out toward the door.

"Hold on a minute, where did George come from?" Emmett asked, stepping in her path. Aria raised her brows at him.

"There is no time to explain," she said firmly. "But trust me. When I get my hands on him, he's going to wish he never came back."

Emmett stepped aside and followed her out of the castle. "I'm going with you," he said, not caring whether or not she agreed.

Aria inclined her head. "I was counting on it." She raised her hands, her mind clear as a summer's day, and let the cold shoot out, creating a winged horse made of ice. It snorted and jumped into life, neighing at her.

"You think you could make me one of those?" Emmett asked. But Aria laughed lightly.

"Oh no," she said, and Emmett's face dropped. "You need something bigger." Aria waved her arms and formed a huge ice dragon. It pulled back its neck, rising on two giant legs, and roared. A spray of ice-cold cloud emitted from its jaws, and Emmett shivered.

"A dragon? Are you serious?" he said, his teeth chattering.

Aria mounted her horse and raised a palm at the dragon. "It has wings. That's all that matters."

Emmett climbed on the back of the dragon. "Okay, Roger, lead the way!"

CHAPTER NINETEEN

*E*mmett had never ridden a dragon before, let alone one made of ice. But it wasn't a slippery ice; it was dry and with enough texture that made it easier to hold a firm grip. He tried not to look down as the dragon sped over the snow-covered trees of the Chanted Forest. But then the trees ended, and the dragon flew past the beach and toward the ocean, which had scattered blocks of ice bobbing over the dark waters.

Emmett wasn't entirely sure what caused the sudden winter, but if he had to guess, The Snow Queen had an emotional meltdown when she found out her sister had been taken. He glanced at Aria as she rode on her winged horse next to him, but something was strange about her. Her demeanor was focused but the flush of her cheeks made her appear more emotional. Or maybe knowing that Snow was at the hands of a man who wanted her all to himself was filling her with hot rage that was impossible to hide.

Emmett couldn't quite blame George for feeling that way. And if Snow had willingly gone with him out of her own free will, Emmett wouldn't even have thought twice about letting her go. She deserved to be happy. But taking her while she was unconscious? That was unacceptable. Even if they had been together in days past.

In the distance, Emmett noticed an island with a tower made of rocks in the center. It looked small at first, but it grew larger as they got closer. Emmett couldn't understand how on Earth George could have gotten there so quickly. Surely he didn't have a winged crea-ture to fly them there.

Or did he?

Aria waved a hand, and the ice dragon slowed, soaring up higher in the air. By the concerned look on Aria's face, Emmett could tell something was wrong. Her brows were furrowed with sharp focus, but something about her constant glances toward the water made it seem like a prey sensing its predator.

Emmett leaned sideways, leading the dragon to soar closer to Aria. "What's wrong?" he asked.

"He's here," she said, sensing something in the air.

"Probably in that tower." Emmett pointed ahead.

"No…" Aria raised a hand as if somehow she could silence the world. "*Here*." She looked down.

Just as Emmett followed her gaze, a monstrous creature with the head of a dragon jumped out of the water. It was ten times the size of a dolphin, with four gnarly limbs and a long tail with razor-sharp scales. It head-butted the ice dragon, causing it to shatter. With nothing to hold onto, Emmett fell into the ocean like a scrambling bug. The freezing water felt like knives piercing through his body. When he broke the surface and took a greedy gulp of air, the monster collapsed into the water in a bellyflop, creating a wave so huge,

Emmett held his breath and dove under again. The wave crashed over him, and he swam to the surface.

A gray, iridescent fin appeared to his left, and he hurried to grab one of the chunks of icebergs floating in the water. Just as he climbed onto it, the monster's tail rose above him and crashed it down on the edge of the ice, sending Emmett flying through the air and splashing back into the water.

The freezing liquid engulfed him, sending a sharp stab into his brain. When he came up for air, he caught Aria flying above, shooting daggers of ice at the water dragon.

"George!" Aria yelled. "If you don't surrender my sister, I will make you regret it!"

The monster was George?

The creature screeched as he hurled his tail toward Aria. Ice exploded from her palms, freezing the tail in midair. She continued to freeze the rest of his body, immobilizing his back, then all around him until he was trapped inside giant walls of ice.

Sensing his opportunity to go to the tower, Emmett wasted no time climbing onto another piece of iceberg while the creature was trapped. He hopped from one iceberg to another, getting closer and closer to the island where the tower stood.

The water dragon let out a piercing cry, then spikes poked out of his back, shattering the ice until he was free again. Broken fragments of ice rained down into the water. He turned around with his black eyes locked on Emmett.

Undeterred from his goal, Emmett pushed his legs harder, jumping as high as he could manage. He glanced over his shoulder and spotted Aria creating walls of ice in the water dragon's path. He slowed down after each impact. But then he dove underwater, and an eerie silence followed.

Emmett stopped and swung around. Aria swooped down with her winged horse, but instead of grabbing him out of harm's way, she dropped her satchel at his feet, then flew past him.

Emmett hurried to look inside, and immediately he knew what Aria was suggesting. He lifted his eyes and caught the dragon's spikes cutting through the water toward him. He crouched on top of the iceberg and braced himself, waiting for the aquatic monster to draw closer. When he finally leaped out of the water with his teeth bared, Emmet sucked in a deep breath and jumped into the water. The freezing temperature was like daggers piercing into his skin, but he forced himself to focus on the task. He looked up to find the dragon swimming over him. He touched the dragon's belly, then grabbed his small legs, bracing himself as he was pulled at an incredible speed.

Without another thought, he shoved his hand into the satchel, pulled out the genie bracelet, and clamped it on the dragon's ankle like a shackle. The water dragon roared so loudly, the water trembled around Emmett. He lost his grip and swam back to the top. When his head broke through the surface, he took the most desperate gasp of air. His lungs ached as his heavy breathing created a puff of flurries in front of his face. Then another human broke through the surface next to him, gasping for air and flailing his arms in a surge of panic.

Emmett looked up to find Aria swooping down on her winged horse again. He reached to grab human George, hooking his arm around his chest, then took Aria's outstretched arm with his other hand.

She snatched them out of the water like an eagle snatching its food, then flew them toward the island about a hundred feet away. As soon as she dropped them on the snow, George staggered to his feet and ran naked past Emmett, disappearing into the island's forest.

Aria landed her winged horse on the sand and jumped down with balled fists and a scowl.

Emmett pushed himself to his knees, panting. "Aria—"

"Go get my sister," Aria hissed, glaring into the woods. "I'll handle *him*."

Emmett nodded, not bothering to argue. He staggered to his feet and mounted the winged horse, letting it take him up to the top of the tower. As he looked in through the open window, he saw a casket of ice sitting in the center of an empty room. Emmett jumped on the rocky ledge of the window, then slowly entered the room. As he drew closer, Snow's beautiful face came into view. He stopped next to the casket and pushed the top out of the way. It slid off and shattered on the rocky floor.

Slowly, he knelt down and allowed his heartbeat to return to normal as he stared at Snow's pretty rosebud lips and her thick lashes. She lay so peaceful and still.

Emmett frowned. "What did they do to you?"

He leaned over Snow and brushed a strand of black hair from her porcelain face. He watched her for a long moment, knowing that only true love's kiss would bring her back. He had no doubt in his mind that his love for her was true, but what if she didn't feel the same way? What if she still loved George? After all, she wasn't able to see what a monster he'd become.

An ache rose in Emmet's chest at the mere thought of her heart belonging to someone else. But there was only one way to find out. He brushed his thumb over her rosy cheek, watching as her red lips beckoned to him.

Without another thought, he leaned in and pressed his lips gently to hers.

CHAPTER TWENTY

$\mathcal{A}$ ria tore through the forest, not stopping to even take a breath as she followed the fresh footsteps in the snow. The genie bracelet had suppressed George's ability to shift, and the cold would slow him down. Aria had the upper hand.

Foliage whipped at her as she ran, and as a thorny branch sliced her arm, she didn't even flinch. Adrenaline coursed through her veins. She ran faster than she'd ever run, taking quick breaths and focusing on the rustling bushes up ahead. George was slowing down.

"Stop, George, and face me like man!" Aria shouted. But he wasn't going to stop because he knew she didn't want to talk. She wanted to look him in the eye and slice an ice dagger through his chest and watch the lights fade from his eyes just as he had done with Jack's grandfather.

She still couldn't believe George killed the old man in cold blood, but that wasn't the reason Aria wanted him dead. If he had stepped through the mirror and they talked things out, Aria would've understood. Maybe she would've even apologized for what she'd done while her heart was frozen. But he crossed a line when he took Snow while she was unconscious. And if Aria found out that he touched one hair on her sister's head, his fate would be worse than death.

Grandfather had told her George was a villain. A monster. That was exactly why she pushed him off that balcony and banished him from the Chanted Kingdom. Now she knew what he was capable of and had every bit of the evil running through his veins that his mother possessed.

Finally, Aria found George crouching by a river, wrestling with the shackle around his ankle. As Aria stepped out, he swiveled to see her and balled his hands into fists.

"You just wait until I get this off," he said in a growl. "I'm going to drown you!" But his scowl couldn't hide the fear in his eyes. He was weak. He had always been weak. Even as children, she always fought better than he did. She couldn't believe she'd been friends with someone capable of killing another human in cold blood. Even The Snow Queen, on her worst day, never killed anyone herself. Until now.

Even with her heart no longer frozen, Aria couldn't bring herself to care about his life. Other than her sister's safety, she didn't care about anything anymore. Except for one thing: George had to die. There was only room for one villain in this forest, and in order for Snow to be safe, George could not be allowed to live.

George's eyes flashed red as she approached like a cheetah stalking its prey.

"You did this to me," he hissed. "I never would have become what I am if you hadn't sent me to that wretched world."

"Oxford is hardly wretched," Aria replied. Jack only ever said great things about it.

"Oxford?" George echoed, wagging a finger at her. "You didn't send me to Oxford."

Aria's brows lifted. This was news to her. She had no idea there were places other than Oxford in that realm. "You were in Jack's grandfather's study just now. That was in Oxford."

"I know," George said, his face twisting. "Jack told me about his grandfather after my mother was killed. So, when I realized where I was, I searched for the old philosopher and found him in Oxford. But that was not where I woke up."

Aria didn't bother to cut him off. She was mildly curious to know his story. Where did he go?

"When I fell into the Lake of Reason, I resurfaced in the freezing waters of Loch Ness."

Aria cocked her head and wondered if George thought that would mean anything to her. When she didn't speak, George frowned at her more deeply. "I was... shocked. Scared. Angry." He hugged his naked body and shivered. "The anger was so strong, I started to have blackouts."

Aria dropped her hands. "Blackouts?"

George nodded. "I was in Scotland. A kind family found me washed up on the shoreline, and whispers of a monster flooded the small village by the loch. It wasn't until months later that I realized the Loch Ness monster the people kept talking about... was me."

George's pink cheeks were a stark contrast to his pale, shivering body. She pulled off her cloak and threw it to him. "Wrap yourself up," she barked. George huddled in the cloak with a grumble. "Why did you kill Jack's grandfather?"

"I met him briefly after my mother was killed," George said. "What you don't know is that I overheard his conversation with you in the library before he left. I heard him talk about The Snow Queen and her role as a villain to restore the happy endings. I didn't agree with any of that, but I also couldn't find time alone with you. To talk you out of it. Next thing I know, you were pushing me off that balcony and banishing me to another realm."

Aria watched George for several beats. "So you killed him because...?"

"He had the books," George hissed. "So, I figured that without him and his precious books, you couldn't restore anyone's happy endings anymore. And if I can't have my happy ending, then no one will."

"Do you honestly not even feel any ounce of regret for what you've done?"

"Did *you*? When you killed my mother?" George spat at her feet.

"I didn't kill your mother. Jack did. But no, I don't regret it. She burned men, women, and children alive. She destroyed more villages out of a fit of rage than anyone, and the world is better off without her."

George hissed, seething at her words. "And you're any better? On your own coronation day, you tossed me over that balcony like I was an unwanted rat."

"You *are* an unwanted rat."

George's face twisted and he rose to a stand, his hands trembling with anger. "I protected Snow when you ran away, leaving your family to die."

"You call locking her up in a wine cellar

protection?" Aria snapped. "If you really wanted to protect her, you would've taken her far away from your mother and let go. Let her live her life in freedom."

"She was mine!" George hissed, his eyes so wide, it looked like he'd lost his mind. "And she will always be mine, you hear me? Nothing is going to keep me away from her."

Grandfather was right. George had a dark heart. He had masked it well at the beginning, but now the true George faced her, with nothing hidden, and all that Aria saw was ugliness. And pure evil.

George stood, then took a menacing step toward Aria. "When I get this off, I'm going to enjoy ripping you from limb to limb. And I'll do it slowly."

Aria lifted a brow. "I'd like to see you try."

His eyes flashed with anger, and he spun around to run again.

Aria rolled her eyes, losing patience. She shot two blasts of ice, plastering George's arms to a tree. He wrestled and grunted, trying to break free as Aria approached.

"I hate you," he spat at her again. "I hope someone cuts off your head."

Aria raised a hand and formed a large ice sword. "You know, I was deliberating on how to kill you. Thank you for the inspiration."

She swung the sword behind her with both hands, and George shut his eyes, bracing for impact. When she dragged the heavy sword through the air, a ferocious wind stopped it just before it reached George's neck.

"Aria, don't."

Aria dropped the sword at the whisper in the wind, and it shattered at her feet. She turned, blinking into the wind until she found him. A tall man with snowy white hair and a long, white cloak walked toward her. For a moment, Aria thought she had somehow been killed and was sent to another realm entirely. But then she met his eyes, they were glacier blue at first, but as the winds dyed down, they turned brown and bore deep into her soul.

"Jack," she whispered. Time stood still, and Aria stopped breathing as she laid eyes on the love of her life. Hardly believing him to be there. It surely was a cruel trick.

Jack stopped a few feet from her and nodded to George, who was still pinned to the tree. "You don't have to be the villain, Aria. You can make a different choice."

Aria looked at George, who stared at Jack with his mouth hanging open. "You don't understand." She looked back at Jack, trying to sound warm, but it was surprisingly diffi-cult. "George killed your grandfather. He did it right before my eyes."

Jack blinked a few times as he studied George.

"I'm not going to apologize if that's what you're waiting for," George spoke through gritted teeth, his forehead reddening.

Jack shut his eyes and bowed his head, his mouth forming a thin line. But then his face relaxed and he looked at Aria with sadness in his eyes. "It doesn't matter. Aria, you're not a killer. This isn't who you are."

"I'm not the same person I was when you left, Jack," Aria said. Then she formed an ice dagger and turned to George, resolute. "And it's better this way."

Jack stepped in her path, and the ice dagger hovered over his chest. "Is it really better? Are you happy with who you've become?"

"I'm a villain, Jack. You know very well this was never about my happiness."

"You're not a villain, Aria. A real villain doesn't have to freeze her own heart in order to be evil. Only a good person does. You're a good person." He reached out and grazed her cheek with his thumb. "And I'm so sorry I left you. I should have stayed. I see that now."

His warmth landed on Aria like the rising sun, and her frozen soul splintered. But she shook her head and looked at George, anger seeping through the cracks. "Every story needs a villain. It's just the way it works."

"That's exactly why you need to let him go," Jack whispered, and Aria returned her gaze to his eyes. They grew misty, and her heart squeezed so tightly, she could hardly breathe. "Let *him* be the villain so you can be free."

"But your grandfather said—"

"My grandfather was wrong," Jack insisted. "He was wrong about a lot of things."

"But not about this," Aria replied. "Not about the happy endings. I read the books. I saw their destiny—"

"Destiny is not a good thing," Jack replied. "It takes away the person's freedom of choice. The Intruder might've shifted the stories when he meddled in people's lives, but he didn't ruin their happy endings. People can still choose to be happy without following the book."

Aria gave Jack a quizzical look. "What do you mean?"

"It means that in the books, Red never marries the wolf. The Snow Queen doesn't fall in love with Jack Frost. And Snow doesn't love the Huntsman," Jack explained. "None of their stories played out like the originals, but yet, they've all found true love."

"But your grandfather never told me—"

"Because he wanted you to keep going," Jack explained. "He wanted you to keep being the evil Snow Queen."

"But why?"

"Because you were the only villain he could control. And my grandfather was obsessed with fixing his mistake. He was obsessed with a lot of things. But he's gone now. And you can be free. So, what do you say?"

Aria held Jack's gaze, trying to think of an

argument, but when she couldn't think of anything, she sighed and aimed her palm at George. He broke free, and without a word, turned on his heels and ran away.

"Now what?" she asked Jack, looking around them. Everything was white, and icicles hung from the glistening frozen branches of the trees. The frosty lake sparkled in the weak sunlight, pouring through the white clouds above.

Then she remembered the shockwave, sending everything into an eternal winter. "I don't know how to fix this," she said.

Jack took her hand, and the gentle touch gave her goosebumps. "Aria," he whispered.

She raised her eyes to meet his tender gaze.

"My darling Aria." He brushed her hair away from her face. "It's taken me some time to come to terms with what I've become. When I left, I thought I was doing the right thing, but you needed me, and by leaving you, I walked away from who I really am."

He took her face in his hands, and Aria's chest pinched. "I... I missed you," she whispered. "If my heart hadn't been frozen, I don't think I would've survived without you." She bit her lip at the confession, but Jack smiled so warmly, it burned into her.

"Why are you smiling?" she asked, her brows furrowing. "I just told you my heart was frozen, which meant I couldn't love you anymore."

Jack pressed his forehead against hers and sighed, his breath warming her cheeks. "Freezing your heart was the greatest sacrifice you could do, and if that isn't an act of love, I don't know what is."

Aria's body heated as Jack closed the gap between them and his chest pressed against hers. He found her waist and ran his hands up her back as if to warm her heart again.

With every lingering look and brazen touch, her heart responded with a flutter.

"From now on, we work together," Jack said, his voice steady. He pressed his lips to her forehead, and Aria bit her lip as a rush of emotion flooded through her veins.

"Promise you will never leave me again?" she whispered, the ice around them melting away. Jack wrapped her up in his arms and buried his face in her neck, holding her so tightly, Aria could hardly catch a breath.

"Never again," he said softly. "You are my destiny. We were always meant to be together, and for as long as I live, you'll always have me by your side." He lifted his head, and the last of the ice dripped away.

Aria's heart throbbed so hard, it sent a gush of tears to her eyes. "You promise?" she breathed.

Jack didn't answer with words. Instead, he grabbed the back of her neck and found her mouth with his. The kiss lit up every part of Aria's mind like fireworks. As she dragged her hands up to his hair, succumbing to the kiss, her heart soared, exploding with such intensity, it sent another shockwave through her core. This time was more intense and powerful than before as it blasted from her body and into the atmosphere.

Jack and Aria broke apart and looked around in wonderment as a tremendous gust of wind took over the forest. All the ice and snow evaporated, giving way to lush green grass and blooming trees. The blossoms flooded the air with their floral scent and the skies cleared, giving way to glorious sunshine. Aria turned back to Jack, beaming. "My heart…" she said through tears.

Jack placed his hand gently over it. "…Is pure again."

Aria bit her lip. "How can you say that, after all I've done?"

Jack kissed her, grazing his lips tenderly over hers, and nuzzled her cheek. "I don't know anyone who would be willing to sacrifice everything just so everyone else can get their happy endings."

Aria closed her eyes, tears sliding down her cheeks. She opened them again, checking that this wasn't a dream. Jack squeezed her hand as though to reassure her. "Now, isn't it about time you get yours too?"

CHAPTER TWENTY-ONE

Snow opened her eyes, blinking into the bright light. Then, to her surprise, Emmett's face came into view as he hovered over her.

She sat up, her mind dull. "What... happened? I thought you left," she said, touching her lips. She couldn't be sure if it was her imagination, but she thought Emmett had kissed her. "Where are we?"

One minute she was talking to Aria by the lake, enjoying an apple, then the next she was waking up in a strange place, walking aimlessly along a vast countryside. She wandered for hours through the misty fields, her mind confused. But then she fell into darkness again and found herself waking up with Emmett leaning over her.

"I came back for you," he said, lifting her from the glass bed and cradling her in his arms. Snow wrapped her arms around his neck and looked around. Suddenly, nothing else mattered. Emmett had come back.

"Does this mean... you forgive me?" she asked, hardly daring to hope.

Emmett let her down and took her hands in his. "We've both done things we're not proud of," he said sincerely. "But I know I'm a better person when I'm with you. And if you'll have me, I'm sure we will spend the rest of our lives making better choices... together."

Snow held on to Emmett's shoulders and squeezed.

"I love you, Snow," he whispered, and her heart skipped a beat.

Snow threw caution to the wind and placed her hands on his cheeks. "I love you more," she whispered. Then she leaned in and kissed him, with every ounce of her body buzzing. Emmett scooped her up in his arms again and lifted her into the air, their lips still joined.

Just as Snow's mind grew dizzy, an owl hooted. They broke away from each other to watch Roger swoop in between them and settle on Snow's shoulder, nuzzling her neck and ruffling his feathers.

Snow giggled as she stroked his smooth, feathered back.

"He's your true hero," Emmett said, crossing his arms with a broad grin.

Snow kissed Roger's head. "Thank you, Roger."

Roger hooted. *Thank goodness you're alive. Come outside, you won't believe who's here.*

A chuckle greeted Snow as she emerged from the bottom of the tower with Emmett. She looked up and held her breath at the sight of Jack and Aria walking toward them hand in hand.

"You came!" she cried, running to Jack and throwing her arms around him for a hug. Jack laughed into her hair, and when she pulled back, she sensed something had changed in him. He was warmer than before. Like he had a part of his humanity back. Then she looked at Aria, who smiled at her, her face brimming with happiness.

"Hey Emmett, I wonder if you could help me with something? I understand you're a talented huntsman," Jack said, shooting the women a look before smiling at Emmett. Snow would normally argue against hunting, but she knew Jack was just trying to give her and Aria some space.

Emmett looked at her, hesitating. "Go, we'll catch up in a minute," she said reassuringly. Emmett nodded and followed Jack into the forest.

When they disappeared in the tree line, Aria pulled Snow in for a tight hug. "George is back," she said as they broke apart.

Snow's mouth fell open, but she was surprised that the news did not make her feel any ounce of joy.

Aria looked down. "He killed Jack's grandfather and then he took you to this tower."

Snow looked up at the stone tower with angry waters surrounding them. "George killed…?" Her head ached as she tried to fathom what had happened.

"I'll explain everything to you later, but right now, I thought you should know that I'm not going to be the villain anymore," Aria said, her cheek dimpling. But then her smile faded. "I'm so sorry for everything you've been through."

Snow hugged her sister so tight. "You were right. About it all. I mean, I had no idea George could be so..."

"Evil?" Aria finished for her.

Snow rubbed her arm. "I guess the apple doesn't fall far from the tree," she said, thinking about his mother being The Evil Queen. "And Emmett came back. So, I guess you have nothing to be sorry about. It all worked out in the end."

Aria's face brightened, but then she bit her lip, troubled.

"What's wrong?" Snow asked.

Aria looked away, frowning. Then she turned back to Snow again. "There's some-thing else you need to know."

Snow wondered what could be bigger than the news she already told her.

Aria tucked a strand of hair behind her

ear and took her sister's hands. "You are the rightful queen of the Chanted Kingdom."

Snow swallowed, stunned as the news landed. But then she shook her head. "No, I found out the truth on the Ice Mountains. I'm…"

"The baby you saw…" Aria said. "It wasn't you."

Snow squinted at her sister and cocked her head to the side. But Aria wasn't done. "It was me. I was adopted by our parents, which makes you the rightful heir to the throne."

Snow's breath hitched. "You're…"

"Part-flipping-mermaid. I know." Aria shut her eyes with a huff. "I'm not happy about it either."

Snow broke into a giggle. For all these years, Aria had hated mermaids. Now, she was one of them. Snow imagined how that news must have been received.

"I don't care about where you came from," Snow said, opening her arms wide. "We'll always be sisters."

Aria hugged her sister again, breathing into her hair. "Always."

CHAPTER TWENTY-TWO

Snow's heart beat faster than the wings of a hummingbird as Aria helped her into the long white gown. She had offered the maids to assist her, but Snow insisted she wanted her sister to help her. Especially when she saw the dress and eyed it with a mixture of wonderment and trepidation.

The lace overlay had birds and butterflies embroidered along the skirt, which poofed out with so much material that the dress weighed heavier than a dwarf in her arms. But the dress wasn't the reason Snow didn't want anyone around. After several minutes of hobbling on one foot, grunting and struggling with the gown, Aria—who had been waiting outside—walked in and helped her climb into it.

The gown fit Snow like a glove. The boning in the bodice held everything in place, and Aria fastened the fifty small loop buttons all down her back.

Snow admired her dark hair fixed up with daisies and two sunflowers, thinking that she should wear flowers in her hair more often. She turned and pressed a finger in a rosy-red paste, then dabbed it on her lips and blended a little on her cheeks until she had rose-red lips and a hint of blush to her complexion.

Roger looked on from the windowsill. He was unusually quiet. Perhaps he was groggy from being woken up so early, or maybe he was simply replaying their adventures together, wondering how Snow was now all grown up, getting married and on her way to ruling a kingdom. It was hard for Snow to comprehend it all, as well.

Snow looked up at the long wall mirror of ice that Aria had made for her. The frame had intricate designs of snowflakes and birds. As

Snow looked at her reflection, she almost couldn't recognize the woman staring back.

She had once been so unsure of herself, so worried and fearful of the future. Having lived years in hiding, being told she was too weak to fight for her kingdom, the woman looking back in the mirror told an entirely different story.

Now, she was a queen. There would be no more hiding. No more questioning of her worth or ability. Unlike her successors, she would rule with a pure heart and let kindness and charity guide her decisions. The Chanted Kingdom deserved that. After all the horrors that people have had to endure.

Aria hummed, as though she heard Snow's thoughts, and squeezed her upper arms, making eye contact through the mirror. "You will be the most loved queen the Chanted Kingdom has ever known," she said with reverence.

Snow placed a hand over Aria's and smiled. "They will come to love you too, once everyone learns of your sacrifice."

Aria pulled her hand away, looking troubled.

Snow turned and looked at her. "George was the villain this time, not you," she said firmly. "He murdered Jack's grandfather in cold blood, he took me to a deserted tower, and I could only imagine what other atrocities he had planned if you hadn't saved me."

Aria looked at the floor with her brows pinched. "He only became the villain because of what I did to him." Her face screwed up in anger. "Now, he's out there, alive and… and… all alone, and I'm afraid for him. He may have lost his mind, but he was my friend, Snow. What if I turned him into a monster?"

Snow held Aria's hand and squeezed it tightly. "Our relationship was never an equal partnership. He convinced me that I was weak and unable to take care of myself. He knew what his mother was… what she did to the villages. Never once did he try to stop her. Not once did he accept that she did terrible things."

Aria pulled Snow in for a gentle hug, and the two sisters stayed like that for a breath. The birdsong floated in through the open window, and when it picked up, Snow could just make out the words.

Snow and Emmett are getting married today.
Hip, hip, hooray! Hip, hip, hooray!
Snow and Emmett are our queen and king,
Shout out hooray! Come along and sing!

The birds sang the four lines on a loop, the excitement growing each time, and as Snow pulled away from Aria, she couldn't stop herself from smiling.

"Don't worry about George," she said, giving Aria a firm look. "He might be a villain now, but there are more heroes in this kingdom than he can handle."

When Aria's eyes turned sad, Snow tilted her head to the side. "You're not staying, are you?"

Though it might have been naive, Snow had envisioned a future where she and Emmett and Jack and Aria lived happily in the castle together, and that Snow would rule with the occasional advice from her sister, and Jack, who had become wise beyond most humans in their lifetime.

"Jack said I could learn so much more about my powers at the Ice Mountains," Aria said, her smile growing. "He also thinks my mother came from that tribe, just like his family."

Snow frowned, but Aria shook her head, picking up on Snow's thoughts. "But if you ever need me, for anything at all, I'll be here in a heartbeat."

Snow pulled in a deep breath as a pair of bluebirds flew over, holding her veil in their claws. They lowered the dainty tiara to her hair and Snow thanked them.

She turned back to Aria. Her white-blonde hair was in a braid over her left shoulder with strands of hair flowing freely, framing her face. She wore a simple dress, a light shade of blue, and for the first time in a long time, she did not have a worry line between her brows. Her face radiated happiness, and there was a wholeness to her that wasn't there before.

Most people probably wouldn't recognize The Snow Queen with a beaming smile on her face, but to Snow, that was her sister. Not the villain Jack's grandfather had made her become. Snow believed in her when no one else did, and it was worth every sweat, blood, and tear. Aria was happy again and healed. If Snow was able to save her sister, she was confident she would be strong enough to rule and be the kind of queen her kingdom needed her to be.

Though Aria was still concerned about George coming back, Snow wasn't. She had no idea if the son of The Evil Queen would ever come back and try to take her again, one thing was certain...

If he ever returned, Snow would be ready.

CHAPTER TWENTY-THREE

*E*mmett had never heard so many birds singing at once. The Chanted Forest began beaming with life at sunrise, and it hadn't stopped since. He sucked in a nervous breath as he stood in the garden under a gazebo made of flowers.

A strong hand patted his back, and he turned around to find his brother with a proud smile. "Don't lock your knees," he said. "It might make you faint."

Emmett nodded. "Thanks."

"Who would've thought," Nathaniel said, still smiling. "You become king once more."

Emmett gave his brother a sincere look. "No I'm not. I'll continue to be known as

Prince Emmett, and I'll spend the rest of my days supporting my Queen."

"How much longer is this going to take?" Robin approached holding a small silver bottle in his hand. "I'm starving."

"Where's my sister?" Emmett asked.

"She's with the rest of the girls fixing up your bride," Robin replied, offering Emmett the flask. "Here."

Emmett arched a dark brow. "What is that?"

"For the nerves."

Robin didn't have to say any more. Emmett chuckled.

"No thanks."

"Suit yourself," Robin said with a shrug. But then he fell silent and looked around the palace as if he was seeing everything for the first time. "Can I ask you both a question?"

Nathaniel and Emmett looked at him, intrigued. Robin wasn't usually careful with his words. If he had something to say, he said it.

"Do you think your sister would prefer a wedding like this?" When he turned to the brothers, he seemed genuinely interested in their advice. Maybe even a slight hint of concern in his eyes. "I mean, she is a princess."

"Marian knows where you come from," Nathaniel replied. "She chose you because of what you have to offer, not for the things you lack. So, I'm sure that whatever you give her, as long as it's from your heart, she will love it."

Robin looked at Emmett. "Do you have anything to say?"

"Nope." Emmett popped his lips for emphasis. "I've learned the hard way not to make decisions for my sister. So, if you really want to know what she wants... ask her."

Robin let out a long breath. "It's just that she deserves the world, you know?"

Emmett smiled, then clapped Robin's back. "My sister doesn't want the world. If she did, she would've married Prince John. She just wants you."

Roger flew from the castle's balcony and landed on top of the gazebo. He didn't have to hear Roger speak to understand what he was saying. Snow was ready and on her way. Emmett squared his shoulders and adjusted his tie.

Belle and his sister walked out of the castle, giggling and gushing down the steps with their own bouquets of flowers in hand, then made their way to the front row and took a seat next to the seven dwarfs. Robin settled next to Marian as she beamed at the groom. Emmett gave a wink to mask his nerves, but when the orchestra began to play, he gulped and clasped his hands behind his back

His brother put a calming hand on his shoulder and gave it a hard squeeze. It was such a simple gesture, but it was enough to comfort him. Snow had already been crowned the new queen, and he would indeed become king, but today, she was just his sweet and kind Snow. And he was just a man marrying his true love.

The double doors opened, and all the guests rose to their feet. Aria stepped out, holding a bouquet of red and yellow roses. She descended the stone steps and walked down the aisle until she reached Emmett. She curtsied to him, and he bowed his head. She then went to stand to his left, and he focused on the double doors again.

The moment Snow stepped outside, her

eyes locked with Emmett's. Her dark hair sat in soft curls to her shoulders and posed a stark contrast to the lacy, white dress sparkling in the sunshine. Red, yellow, and white cardinals flew behind her and a line of bluebirds lifted the train of her dress, all the while chirping happily. She looped her hand in Jack's arm and, together, they descended the steps. When she beamed, Emmett smiled back. It didn't fade until she was finally standing in front of him. The colorful birds lowered her train, then elegantly lifted her veil over her head.

Jack brought Snow to Emmett, where they stood beneath an arch adorned by an array of spring flowers. They turned to face each other. When their eyes met, there was no doubt in Emmett's mind that Snow was his true love. By the time he was asked to share his vow, his heart overflowed with love for the woman standing in front of him.

He took her hands in his and watched her for a moment. "Snow..." A gentle smile spread across his face. "You are everything I'm not. And yet, you're everything I need. My heart has suffered more loss than most, and for that alone, I didn't think the void inside me could ever be filled. I was too broken. Too empty. But then I met you..." He gave her hands a light squeeze. "You patched every crack in my heart. Soothed every wound. Healed every scar. You filled me with hope until the void was gone. I am a new man today because of you, and I look forward to spending the rest of my life being the best version of myself... just for you."

Snow's eyes turned glassy with tears, but she pressed her red lips together, trying not to cry. "Emmett..." She watched him for a moment. "All my life I've hidden in the background. Allowed others to rise above me. But you..." She smiled. "You saw a side of me that even I never knew existed. You believed in me when everyone else had given up. You pushed me to be better. You challenged me in ways that were both thrilling and uplifting. But, most importantly... you taught me that *true* strength comes from within. And that *love* is the most powerful weapon of all. With you, I am the strongest version of myself, and I vow to spend the rest of my days loving you—"

Emmett pressed his lips to hers with such an urgency, she let out a little surprised gasp against his mouth. He knew it wasn't time yet, but he couldn't contain the urge. The pull toward her, to *taste* her, was too strong. Her red lips molded against his. It was sweet as an apple, and her cheeks were soft as he gently brushed his thumbs over them.

He pulled back and opened his eyes slowly as light chuckles came from the wedding guests. Though he paid no attention to them, for he could not take his eyes off her lips that were still perked as if beckoning him to continue.

"Sorry," he whispered. "You were saying...?"

Snow gave him a lopsided grin, then threw her arms around his neck. "Oh, Emmett. Who would've thought a huntsman could be so *charming*?"

EPILOGUE

LEXA

Lexa watched fireworks decorate the sky as she sat on a large rock at the edge of the ocean. Her wet, brown hair cascaded over two white seashells with gray speckles—the only form of clothing to keep her modesty. As was customary for mermaids.

She lowered her eyes to the poultice she mixed in a jar, using a stick, as she had done countless times before.

Hackett, a seagull and friend, landed on the rock next to her, hopping in excitement. *The Chanted Kingdom will have a new queen!* his voice entered Lexa's mind telepathically.

I'm just happy someone dethroned The Snow Queen, Lexa replied.

Isn't she your half-sister? Hackett asked, and Lexa was certain that if the seagull had brows, he would have lifted one. Nonetheless, he cocked his head to the side.

Lexa frowned at him in annoyance. With all the thoughts weighing heavily on her mind, the last thing she needed was to be reminded of her wretched half-sister. Leave it to Hackett to always speak without thinking. She went back to mixing the poultice without dignifying his question with a response.

Hackett hopped on her lap and looked up at her. *Have you spoken to your father?*

Why don't you tell me more about this new queen? Lexa asked, skirting around the question.

Oh, her name is Snow White! he said excitedly, not even noticing she had changed the subject on purpose. *And she's getting married today! Did you know she can also communicate with animals?*

That I've heard.

Lexa didn't know Snow personally, but she knew that anyone would've made a better queen than Aria. Though she was happy to hear that Snow was kinder than most land people. According to Bob--the uptight lobster who also happened to be her father's most trusted advisor--Snow saved him recently from a boiling pot. He was captured and almost made into dinner. She somehow was able to communicate with him and handed him over to her pet owl who then dropped him back into the ocean.

If Lexa had to hear his survival story one more time, she would permanently cover her ears with seashells. Bob already hated the surface and couldn't say enough about how dangerous the humans were. But what about Snow? Wasn't she nice to him? Surely not all humans were bad. He was just paranoid because of her father's disapproval of the land and its people.

Lexa clenched her jaw. Thinking about her father stirred up an anger that she took great effort to suppress. All her life, he forbade her from going to the surface, from interacting with the humans, and yet, he had a child with a human after Lexa's mother died.

All those years, he made her feel like she was odd for being drawn to the land, when in reality, she was being just like him. Though, unlike him, Lexa never got to experience land in full as he had.

Lexa enjoyed the heat of the sun on her face, the fresh air blowing through her hair, and the warm sand between her toes. Even though her father knew she would go to the surface from time to time, he had no idea she had the means to generate legs. Thanks to the stone she traded with Aria, Lexa was able to connect with a stone her mother had given her. The two stones fit together like yin-and-yang, and once joined, it gave Lexa the ability to shift into human form. Even if only for a short time. It was just enough for her to enjoy the island she found in the middle of the sea.

More fireworks of red, white, and green exploded like confetti in the distance, and birds' songs traveled melodically through the swaying trees.

The animals were euphoric with the new queen's wedding, the buzz of excitement flowed through the air, and all life in the Chanted Forest sang and danced with glee.

Lexa had never heard of a human who could communicate with animals, and it was rare for them to honor and praise a human. So, whoever Snow was, she had to be special.

Lexa.

The corners of her mouth twitched at the familiar sound of her best friend. His voice was unmistakable, light, charming, and that night, he was jovial. She turned to find Jinko, her dolphin, appearing on the surface of the water. He was tangled up in a long string of algae that wrapped around his head and nose. Though this did nothing to dampen his happy mood. Lexa tilted her head as she studied him.

Oh, Jinko.

She placed the jar aside, then leaped into the water. *What happened?*

I was being very careful, he said as she untangled him. *But then your father found me and asked about you.*

Lexa gave Jinko a horrified look.

Don't worry, he said. *I had already left your cave. But when I told him I didn't know where you were, I don't think he believed me. We might need to come up with a good story to throw him off our track.*

Despite the seriousness of the situation, Jinko spoke like they were playing a game, and he merely wanted to talk strategy.

Why should I hide from him? Lexa grunted, freeing Jinko from the algae. *He lied to me my whole life.*

Jinko wiggled, then swam around a few times. *He wanted me to tell you that he needed to talk to you. I think he might be ready to tell you the truth.*

He didn't even try to hide the excitement in his voice. Jinko was an optimist, always thinking the best of people, but his optimism was lost on Lexa, especially when it came to her father.

What truth? Lexa's brows furrowed. *That he moved on from my mother with a human woman? Or that I'm related to Aria, out of all people?*

Jinko pushed his nose onto Lexa's cheek. *You did save her life once.*

I did it for Jack, Lexa clarified. *He saved my life, and I could tell he wasn't going to let me save him unless I saved her.*

What about the handsome pirate? Jinko asked with googly eyes. *Why did you save his life?*

The pirate's name was Ryke, and Jinko knew why she had saved his life. He knew that all it took was one look at the pirate with dark hair and piercing blue eyes, and her heart was claimed. She could no longer see a life, or even an existence, without him in it. So, he had to live.

Except, he couldn't stay in her life. That was never going to be part of her reality. Even if she did save his life after the shipwreck and spent weeks nursing him back to health, they could never have a future together. He couldn't live with her under the sea, and she couldn't have legs for more than a few hours in a day. So, the land was not a viable option, either.

A life with him was nothing but a mere dream. One that was coming to an end sooner rather than later.

Do I have a blowfish in my mouth? Jinko asked. *It hurts when I try to swallow.*

He opened his mouth to reveal a large piece of metal curved at an angle, piercing his tongue. *Oh, no. It's a shark fork!* Lexa carefully removed it with a light tug, then held it up.

Why is it called a shark fork? Jinko asked, flipping his head from side to side, as though shaking off the sting on his tongue.

No idea. Lexa turned to the seagull who was still on the rock. *Do you know?*

Why, of course. Hackett hit his beak on the

metal a few times, then cocked his head. *For humans, a fork pierces food. This large one…* He beaked the metal again, *pierces shark food.*

Jinko's eyes grew wide. *Whoa.* Evidently, he was enthused at the idea of almost swallowing such a useful object.

Lexa examined the metal even more carefully. *Interesting.*

It's also a scratcher for whales, Hackett added. *Whales get very scratchy, you see. This nifty gadget does the perfect job at scratching those hard-to-reach areas.*

Lexa sat up on the large, smooth rock again and reached for the jar.

What is that? Jinko asked, nudging her iridescent fin.

It's for Ryke's injury, Lexa answered, holding up the jar, the almost-transparent paste glistening in the sun like diamonds. *He's almost fully healed.*

Her smile faded as a wave of sadness washed over her.

Does that mean he's leaving? Jinko asked, his voice laced with disappointment for the first time.

Lexa shrugged, her face downcast. *It was*

going to happen sooner or later. He couldn't just live on this island forever.

Can you ask him to stay?

Lexa shook her head, but not before smiling briefly at Jinko's naivety. If only it were that simple. *I couldn't do that to him.*

Why not? Jinko asked. *You saved his life. You nursed him back to health.*

It still wouldn't be fair to him, she pressed. *Not when all I have to offer is a couple of hours in a day.*

With true love, all things are possible, right? Jinko countered, resting his head sideways on her lap so he could look up at her.

She smiled and caressed his head. *Not this time, unfortunately.* She let out a long sigh. *Well, I better go find him before my father sends Bob looking for me.*

Jinko sank back into the water, and she reached for her necklace with both mermaid stones hanging on it. She fit them together, and with immediate effect, her tail split in two and transformed into legs.

She let out a giddy laugh, riveted by the feeling of her toes wiggling. Jinko made a cheerful sound as he lifted out of the water and pushed himself backward using his tail like a happy dance.

Lexa stood and turned to Jinko. *I'll see you soon.*

She jumped from the rock to the warm sand with a giddy smile. The feeling of her weight on the ground, held up by two feet and wobbly legs, was unlike anything she'd ever experienced before she got her necklace. Even though she had walked several times, it was still fascinating. She supposed the novelty of having legs might never truly wear off.

She grabbed the bundle of human clothes that she kept hidden by the rock, then reached for a satchel. She shoved the shark fork in the bag along with the jar of poultice. Throwing her bag over her shoulder, she headed for the forest of the island.

On her way toward the other side of the island, she foraged legumes and fruits and shoved them into her bag. From a distance, she spotted Ryke, shirtless and waist-deep in the water, holding a makeshift spear in his hand.

She stopped walking for a moment and watched longingly as drips of water slid down his chiseled back. His strong arm lifted the spear over his head, and that was when she realized what he was about to do.

Fishermen alert! Away from the shore, now!

The fish must've scattered because Ryke lowered the spear, scratching his pitch-black hair. Lexa watched him look around with confusion, as if wondering what just happened.

She smiled, then continued on her way toward him. When he noticed her approaching, a beaming smile spread across his face. He held Lexa captive with his piercing eyes. Her heart thumped so hard, it hurt, but she gritted her teeth and tried to ignore it.

"Hey!" He waved. "Where did you go? I was looking everywhere for you."

She held up her bag. "I went to find some food."

"I was trying to get us some protein, but…" He pointed to the water. "I haven't been able to catch any fish in all the weeks I've been here."

Lexa settled under his makeshift hut, then turned her bag upside down over a thick cloth.

"Chickpeas are a wonderful source of protein."

He walked out of the water. Glistening droplets slid from broad shoulders to his narrow waist. He came to sit next to her, then looked at the pile of legumes and fruits. "What did you get?"

She handed him a papaya. "Have you ever had one of these? They're delicious!"

Ryke arched a brow, and Lexa wondered if that had been a silly question. Did all humans eat papaya? She had only recently discovered it, and Hackett told her it was a fruit only eaten by royal humans... and goats. According to Hackett, papaya was most loved by goats.

Ryke removed the knife from the tip of his spear, then as he was about to cut the fruit, he stared at it for a moment, his brows knitted together.

"Something wrong?" Lexa asked.

He offered her a soft smile. "Such a small thing, but... I can't even hold a fruit."

Lexa lowered her eyes to his left hand. Or lack thereof. He'd lost it during the shipwreck. She'd tried her best to treat it, and although the stump looked a lot better than it did weeks prior—the wound itself was no longer seeping, and a red-raw layer of skin had grown over it. She had a feeling the mental healing would take a lot longer than the physical.

She frowned. "I'm sorry."

He shook his head. "You have nothing to apologize for. If it hadn't been for you, I wouldn't even have survived." He turned to face her, and his blue eyes locked with hers. "And for that, I will be eternally grateful."

Her green eyes dropped to his wet lips, so shiny and smooth, and her stomach fluttered. She looked away and sucked in a nervous breath to steady herself. She had never been attracted to a human before. But whenever she was in Ryke's presence, he made her feel things she didn't even know existed.

"I made something for you," she said, digging into her satchel and pulling out the jar with her own version of a poultice. "It's made with mermaid healing oil. It should help with the scar tissue."

By the time she turned around, Ryke had already sliced the papaya down the middle and was about to grab a chunk with his hand.

"Wait, I have a fork!" She beamed, digging into her satchel again.

"You do?"

She pulled out the large, curved metal attached to a leather handle. "Here…" She handed it to him with a wide smile.

He stared at it, confused. "A hook?"

"It's a shark fork," she added innocently. "But it pierces food just the same. I washed it in the ocean so it's clean, but it might taste a little salty."

An amused smile spread across Ryke's lips. "Thank you."

She smiled. "You're welcome."

He used the curve of the metal to scrape off the seeds from inside of the papaya. After cutting it in small chunks, he used the tip of his knife to pierce the bits of chopped-up fruit.

He fed her a few pieces, and the explosion of sweetness made her eyes roll back. She let out a moan. When her eyes opened again, she caught the look of amusement on Ryke's face as he watched her.

He cleared his throat and devoured the rest as if he hadn't eaten in weeks. But of course he had. She had made sure he got enough nutrition. Though he did look thinner than when she had first brought him there.

Guilt tugged at the pit of her stomach. By that point, she could have taken him to the marina and allowed him to go back home. Even though she'd spent months convincing herself that she wanted him to heal fully, and that mermaid's healing components were a lot stronger than herbs from the land, Lexa knew the real reason she hadn't helped him leave the island was because she wanted to spend more time with him.

That wasn't the case in the beginning, though. After the shipwreck, when she first found him floating in the water surrounded by his own blood, she had to find the nearest piece of land. That was why she brought him to the island. She needed to stabilize him. Several of his ribs had been cracked, he had lost a lot of blood from having lost his hand, and she could tell by the bruises on his body that he had internal injuries. The damage was far too extensive for any human healers to handle.

"What are you thinking about?" Ryke asked as he finished eating.

In the distance, Lexa could see the small wooden boat they built together. It was ready, and she knew he would be leaving soon. She offered him a sad smile, then reached for the jar she had placed aside.

"May I?" she asked, removing the top and scooping the thick paste with four of her fingers.

He placed his forearm on her lap. In silence, she began rubbing the poultice over his scar. Despite the gentle ebb and flow of the waves on the shore, it did little to soothe the pain building up in her heart.

After rubbing the medicinal paste over his scar, she grabbed her cloak and ripped a large chunk of the fabric. She wrapped it around his stump.

"Wait…" Ryke reached for the hook she had given him and shoved it into the cloth. "Go ahead and wrap it around this. Make sure it's tight and secure."

Lexa did as he asked. Once she was done, he lifted it up and examined the hook he had for a hand.

"Not a bad idea," he said, turning to her with a smile. "Thank you."

She tried to smile back, but her heart was too heavy.

"Hey..." He leaned forward and touched her face, rubbing her cheek softly with his thumb. "Don't look at me like that."

"Like what?"

He frowned. "Like you're never going to see me again."

"But the boat's ready and..." She swallowed through the lump in her throat. "You can't stay here forever."

"Then come with me." Ryke's lips barely moved, but the words landed in her heart like a thunderstorm. "Just because you've never been away from this island doesn't mean you should stay here alone."

Another wave of guilt tugged at the pit of her stomach. She had lied to him. But how else was she going to explain being stranded on a deserted island?

His gentle touch on her cheek sent flutters down her spine. "Let me show you the beautiful world that's out there. I promise, you won't regret it."

There was nothing she wanted more than to see the world out there, especially with him by her side, but that couldn't be her reality. "I wish I could."

"What's holding you back?" he asked.

"You wouldn't understand."

"Then help me understand." His deep blue eyes were so intense, she had to look away for fear he might read her thoughts.

"I just can't. I'm sorry." She rose to her feet with her heart aching. "You should just take the boat and go. Go home to your family. To your... whoever else has been waiting for you."

Ryke stood with her. "I'm a pirate," he said, his voice soft and tempting. "There is no one waiting for me. I don't even have a home." He blocked her view of the ocean. His blue eyes glistened in the sun as he watched her. "I have always felt alone in this world... until I met you."

She cupped his face, his scruffy stubble pricking against her palms. Unable to fight against the gravitational pull between them any longer, she leaned in and pressed her lips to his.

A wave of warmth washed over her as his arms wrapped around her waist. He pressed her body against his, and she found his tongue. The sweet taste overtook her senses, and she moaned against his mouth. His strong arms tightened around her, and she wanted that moment to never end. Abandoning her worries and all of the reasons she had that they couldn't be together, Lexa kissed Ryke with every bit of passion she had bottled up for weeks. Suddenly, in his arms, she pushed away every thought screaming in her mind, telling her why she couldn't be with him.

A sudden loud and panicked warning call came from the water, and Lexa ripped herself from Ryke's lips. She turned to the ocean and spotted Jinko jumping out of the water and flipping in the air.

We have to go now! His voice entered her mind like a siren. A stark contrast to his usual upbeat attitude. *It's your father!*

Lexa ran to the shore with the hairs on the back of her neck standing on end, then stopped when her feet hit the water. *What happened?*

Jinko flipped side to side, making a succession of squeaks, the sound he made resembled that of a cry of devastation. Lexa's heart squeezed in her chest.

Your father was taken!

Lexa stopped breathing, and her heart raced even faster. Ryke came to stand next to her and put a hand on her shoulder.

"Are you all right?" he asked, noticing something was wrong.

She stepped away from him and walked farther into the water. Usually she would wait until she was on the other side of the island, and certain that Ryke would not see, before she turned back into a mermaid. But her father was in trouble and there was no time.

"I'm sorry," she whispered, pulling her mermaid stone apart. Within seconds, her iridescent fin appeared, and she slipped into the water.

Ryke jerked back with eyes wide. He stumbled to the ground and gripped the sand as if his mind was spinning. But his eyes never left her as she swam away.

With an aching heart, she gave Ryke one last glance, just in case that was the last time she ever saw him. He opened his mouth to say something, but she had to go.

Lexa turned away and dove into the water with only one other thought in her mind. One urgent thought that overtook all others. As much as her relationship with her father was strained, and though she often complained about him to anyone who might have listened, knowing that he was missing eradicated all other thoughts and emotion. And a deep-rooted need to answer one question, at all costs...

Who could've possibly taken her father?

—*Read Lexa's story in the next installment of Fairytales Reimagined, book 5: Above the Sea. Download Now.*

Made in United States
Orlando, FL
15 July 2025

62977544R00164